ALMOST THERE1, GENTLEMEN. RIGHT ON TIME.2
GOOD. HOW MANY3 ARE THERE WAITING FOR US4?
SEE FOR YOURSELF...5
CAYO ESQUELETO, CUBA
...JUST HIM.
THAT RUNWAY6 LOOKS7 VERY NARROW8. CAN YOU LAND9 IN THIS STORM10?
JUST WATCH ME11, CARLO. BUT BRACE YOURSELVES12, IT'S GONNA GET BUMPY...13
SKYEEEECH

1. On y est presque
2. Pile à l'heure.
3. Combien
4. à nous attendre
5. Vois par toi-même...
6. piste
7. a l'air
8. étroite
9. atterrir
10. tempête
11. Regarde-moi faire
12. accrochez-vous
13. ça va secouer...

THERE.[1] EVERYBODY OK?
WE'RE FINE.[2] AND THERE'S THE GENERAL. MARC, ARE YOU READY[3]?
I THINK SO.
RELAX, MY FRIEND. THERE ARE TWO OF US[4], AND WE'RE BOTH ARMED[5]. HE'S JUST AN OLD MAN.
KEEP THE ENGINE RUNNING.[6] WE DON'T WANT[7] TO STAY A SECOND LONGER THAN WE HAVE TO[8].
SURE. I'LL HAVE TO TURN AROUND[9] BEFORE WE CAN TAKE OFF[10], ANYWAY[11].
GOOD EVENING. YOU HAD NO TROUBLE[12] GETTING HERE?
NONE AT ALL[13], GENERAL.
IS THAT IT?
ONE KILOGRAM OF WEAPONS-GRADE[14] URANIUM. ENOUGH[15] TO DESTROY A CITY.
I WOULD BE INTERESTED TO KNOW WHICH CITY[16] YOU HAVE IN MIND[17].

1. Voilà.
2. C'est bon.
3. prêt
4. On est deux
5. tous les deux armés
6. Laisse tourner le moteur.
7. Inutile
8. de plus que nécessaire
9. faire demi-tour
10. de décoller
11. de toute façon
12. Vous n'avez pas eu de mal
13. Aucun
14. de qualité militaire
15. Suffisant
16. quelle ville
17. vous avez en tête

AND I PAY YOU NOT TO ASK QUESTIONS[1]. YOUR MONEY IS IN THE JEEP. HALF A MILLION[2] DOLLARS, AS AGREED[3].
ABOUT THAT...[4] OUR FRIEND IN MIAMI SENDS HIS APOLOGIES[5], BUT SMUGGLING[6] HAS BECOME MUCH MORE DIFFICULT RECENTLY. THERE WERE EXTRA EXPENSES[7].
A QUARTER[8] OF A MILLION DOLLARS EXTRA[9].
THAT IS UNFORTUNATE[10].
UNFORTUNATE FOR YOU, GENERAL. YOU ARE THE ONE WHO MUST[11] PAY.
I SEE.
I WILL HAVE TO RAISE[12] THE MONEY. I CAN TRANSFER IT TO THE SAME ACCOUNT[13] AS BEFORE[14].
SEE THAT YOU DO.[15] IF IT IS NOT THERE IN THREE DAYS, AMERICAN INTELLIGENCE[16] WILL LEARN WHAT HAPPENED HERE TONIGHT. AND YOUR LITTLE ISLAND WILL NOT BE SO SAFE[17].
GOOD NIGHT, GENERAL.

1. pour que vous ne posiez pas de questions

2. Un demi-million de

3. comme convenu

4. À ce propos...

5. ses excuses

6. la contrebande

7. des frais imprévus

8. Le quart

9. en plus

10. fâcheux

11. C'est vous qui allez devoir

12. Il faut que je réunisse

13. le même compte

14. que la dernière fois

15. Veillez à ce que ce soit fait.

16. les services de renseignements

17. ne sera plus si sûre

GOOD NIGHT, GENTLEMEN. ENJOY YOUR FLIGHT.[1]
LET'S TURN THIS THING AROUND...
HEY, WHAT HAPPENED TO[2] THE LIGHTS?!
IT'S THE GENERAL! HE'S TRYING TO STOP US LEAVING[3]!
WAIT ... THERE YOU GO. PROBABLY[4] JUST THE STORM DISRUPTING THE ELECTRICITY SUPPLY[5].
I'LL FINISH TURNING THE PLANE, THEN WE CAN GO[6].
HURRY. THE SOONER[7] WE ARE IN THE AIR, THE HAPPIER I WILL BE[8].
ALL RIGHT, GENTLEMEN, HERE WE GO[9]. BACK TO[10] CIVILIZATION!
Vrrrrrrr...

1. Bon vol.

2. que s'est-il passé avec

3. de nous empêcher de partir

4. C'est probablement

5. qui crée des coupures de courant

6. et ensuite on s'en va

7. Plus tôt

8. mieux je me porterai

9. c'est parti

10. On retourne à

Rrrrrrrrm
Aaaaaaaa!
Krash!
UNH...
WHAT HAPPENED? YOU DROVE US OFF[1] THE RUNWAY!
I DIDN'T, I SWEAR[2]...
HE TRICKED US![3] THE LIGHTS ... HE MOVED[4] THE RUNWAY LIGHTS SOMEHOW[5]! WE SHOULD NEVER HAVE THREATENED HIM![6] WE'LL DROWN![7]
DON'T BE RIDICULOUS! WE CAN STILL[8] GET OUT ... WE'LL DEAL WITH HIM![9]
AND THEN WE'LL FIND A WAY OFF THIS[10]—

1. Tu nous as fait quitter

2. je le jure

3. Il nous a piégés !

4. Il a déplacé

5. d'une façon ou d'une autre

6. On n'aurait jamais dû le menacer !

7. On va se noyer !

8. encore

9. On va s'occuper de lui !

10. un moyen de se sortir de là

AAAAAAAA!
CROCODILES!
Krunch!
Splash!
AAAAAAH!
"WHICH CITY", INDEED[1]. SUCH...[2]
Krunch!
"...LIMITED MINDS.[3]"

1. non mais
2. Quels...
3. petits cerveaux.

Goooal!
GOOD SHOT[1], ALEX!
I KNEW THERE WAS A REASON[2] I PICKED YOU[3] FOR THE FIRST TEAM[4]!
CHELSEA, LONDON
THANKS, MR WISEMAN. I WON'T LET YOU DOWN[5] WHEN WE PLAY!
I...
ALEX? WHAT'S THE MATTER?[6]
NOTHING, SIR. THIS WON'T TAKE A MINUTE.[7]
BROOKLAND SCHOOL

1. Beau tir

2. Je savais que ce n'était pas pour rien

3. que je t'avais sélectionné

4. équipe

5. Je ne vais pas vous décevoir

6. Qu'est-ce qui se passe ?

7. J'en ai pas pour longtemps.

1. s'entraînait

2. on se promène

3. Laissez tomber

4. Je vous l'ai déjà dit

5. [service de renseignements extérieurs du Royaume-Uni, créé en 1909]

6. collégien

7. espion

8. Cela n'a rien à voir avec

9. société

10. Vraiment.

11. Écoute

12. cela te ferait plaisir

13. au premier rang

14. place

15. tournoi

16. Je siège au comité

17. [nom du club sportif anglais qui organise le tournoi de Wimbledon depuis 1877]

18. Où est le piège ?

19. pas vraiment

20. Laisse-moi t'expliquer.

ALEX! WHAT A SURPRISE! I DIDN'T KNOW YOUR TEAM PRACTISED[1] HERE. BARKER AND I OFTEN WALK[2]—
COME OFF IT[3], MR CRAWFORD, WHAT DO YOU WANT?
I TOLD YOU ALREADY[4], I'M NOT INTERESTED IN MI6[5] ANY MORE. I'M A SCHOOLBOY[6], NOT A SPY[7].
ABSOLUTELY, OF COURSE! NO, I'M ... THIS HAS NOTHING TO DO WITH[8] THE, UM, COMPANY[9].
REALLY.[10]
REALLY! LISTEN[11], HOW WOULD YOU LIKE[12] A FRONT ROW[13] SEAT[14] AT WIMBLEDON?
YOU MEAN THE TENNIS TOURNAMENT[15]?
THAT'S RIGHT. I'M ON THE COMMITTEE[16] OF THE ALL-ENGLAND TENNIS CLUB[17]. I CAN GET YOU IN.
WHAT'S THE CATCH?[18]
THERE ISN'T ONE, NOT REALLY[19]. BUT...
BROOKLAND SCHO
...LET ME EXPLAIN.[20] IT WON'T TAKE A MINUTE.

"LAST WEEK, SOMEONE BROKE IN TO[1] THE MILLENNIUM BUILDING[2] – WHERE THE PLAYERS HAVE THEIR CHANGING ROOMS[3], A GYM, RESTAURANT AND SO ON[4].
"THE INTRUDER DISABLED[5] THE CCTV CAMERAS[6] AND THE ALARM. A THOROUGHLY PROFESSIONAL JOB.[7] WE ONLY KNOW HE WAS THERE AT ALL BECAUSE A SECURITY GUARD SAW HIM LEAVING[8].
"HE WAS A YOUNG CHINESE MAN[9], DRESSED ALL IN BLACK AND WEARING A RUCKSACK[10].
YOU SAID HE WAS[17] A PROFESSIONAL. WHY IS THAT SO STRANGE?
"THE POLICE SEARCHED THE WHOLE CLUB[11] WITH SNIFFER[12] DOGS. THE ANTI-TERRORIST SQUAD[13] WAS THERE FOR[14] THREE DAYS. BUT THEY FOUND NOTHING. WHOEVER IT WAS[15] JUST VANISHED[16]."
IT ISN'T. BUT HE DIDN'T TAKE ANYTHING[18], EITHER[19]! NOT A SAUSAGE![20]
MAYBE[21] THE GUARD DISTURBED HIM[22] BEFORE HE COULD GET HIS HANDS[23] ON WHATEVER IT WAS HE WAS AFTER[24].
NO, HE WAS ALREADY LEAVING WHEN HE WAS SEEN[25].
NOW[26], ISN'T THAT STRANGE?

1. s'est introduit dans
2. [bâtiment construit à Wimbledon, en 2000]
3. vestiaires
4. et cetera
5. a désactivé
6. caméras de télé-surveillance
7. Un vrai travail de pro.
8. l'a vu partir
9. jeune Chinois
10. portant un sac à dos
11. a fouillé tout le club
12. renifleurs
13. section
14. pendant
15. Qui que ce soit, il a
16. disparu
17. que c'était
18. il n'a rien pris
19. non plus
20. Que dalle !
21. Peut-être que
22. l'a dérangé
23. qu'il ne puisse mettre la main
24. qu'il cherchait
25. lorsqu'il a été aperçu
26. Alors

1. Pourquoi voulez-vous que j'aille
2. quelqu'un essaie
3. saboter
4. membres du comité
5. ils n'exercent pas les mêmes activités
6. Tout cela ne tourne pas rond, je trouve.
7. Pourquoi voudrait-on
8. C'est un gros business
9. livres sterling
10. en jeu
11. les contrats de sponsoring
12. les droits de retransmission télévisée
13. les produits publicitaires
14. les personnalités
15. des milliers [de livres]
16. que je fouine
17. Je n'ai vu Wimbledon qu'à la télé
18. j'aimerais beaucoup
19. le court central
20. une visite d'un jour
21. plutôt
22. séjour prolongé
23. en tête

VERY STRANGE. BUT WHY ARE YOU TELLING ME THIS? WHY DO YOU WANT ME TO GO[1] TO WIMBLEDON?
I BELIEVE SOMEONE INTENDS[2] TO SABOTAGE[3] THE TOURNAMENT.
THE OTHER COMMITTEE MEMBERS[4] DON'T BELIEVE ME, BUT THEY DON'T WORK IN THE SAME BUSINESS[5] AS YOU AND I.
IT JUST FEELS ALL WRONG TO ME.[6]
WHY WOULD ANYONE WANT[7] TO SABOTAGE WIMBLEDON?
IT'S BIG BUSINESS[8], ALEX. MILLIONS OF POUNDS[9] ARE AT STAKE[10] - SPONSORSHIPS[11], TV RIGHTS[12], MERCHANDISE[13], VIPs[14] WHO PAY THOUSANDS[15] FOR A TICKET TO THE FINAL...
SO YOU WANT ME TO GO AND SNOOP AROUND[16]. I'VE ONLY EVER SEEN WIMBLEDON ON TV[17], SO I ADMIT I'D LOVE[18] A TICKET FOR CENTRE COURT[19].
BUT I DON'T SEE HOW A DAY'S VISIT[20] IS GOING TO HELP.
OH, IT WOULDN'T. I HAD MORE OF[21] AN...
...EXTENDED STAY[22] IN MIND[23].
BROOKLAND S
KLAND SCHOOL

...JUST JOINING US[1], WE'RE AT A TENSE POINT[2] BETWEEN JACQUES LEFEVRE AND JAMIE BLITZ. LEFEVRE BAGGED THE FIRST TWO[3] SETS AND ONLY NEEDS THIS FINAL GAME[4] TO WIN OUTRIGHT[5]...
...BLITZ, ONE OF THIS YEAR'S[6] HOT FAVOURITES[7], JUST DOESN'T HAVE ANY MORE TO GIVE. HE HASN'T PLAYED ANYWHERE NEAR HIS BEST[8] TODAY...
WIMBLEDON, SIX WEEKS LATER
...AND IT DOESN'T LOOK LIKE[9] HE'S GOING TO RECOVER[10]. THIS WOULD BE THE UPSET[11] OF THE TOURNAMENT.
NOBODY EXPECTED A PLAYER OF BLITZ'S ABILITY[12] TO BE KNOCKED OUT BY—
—BUT THERE IT IS[13]! JACQUES LEFEVRE, THE RANK OUTSIDER[14], HAS BEATEN[15] JAMIE BLITZ IN STRAIGHT SETS[16]! AN EXTRAORDINARY RESULT!
HEY, ALEX! OVER HERE![17]
BLITZ LOOKS ABSOLUTELY BEWILDERED[18] AS HE RETURNS TO[19] THE CHANGING ROOMS...

1. [Pour ceux] qui viennent de nous rejoindre
2. le point est critique
3. s'est emparé des deux premiers
4. ce dernier jeu
5. haut la main
6. de cette année
7. grands favoris
8. du tout au mieux de sa forme
9. il ne semble pas
10. se reprendre
11. revirement
12. du niveau de Blitz
13. c'est fait
14. l'outsider
15. battu
16. en trois manches
17. Par ici !
18. totalement perplexe
19. alors qu'il regagne

1. mauvais match

2. ce qui n'allait pas

3. Il avait l'air d'un somnambule

4. ennuyeux

5. mignon

6. Il a sept ans de plus que toi !

7. Tu t'amuses bien

8. ramasseur de balles

9. en remplacement

10. Ça ne te dérange pas ?

11. que tu files

12. [la Cornouailles, région de la pointe sud-ouest de l'Angleterre]

13. faire du surf

14. On aimerait beaucoup que tu viennes

15. Tu empêcheras Sabina de faire des bêtises.

16. chouette

17. je dois y aller

THAT WAS A REALLY BAD GAME[1]. I DON'T KNOW WHAT WAS WRONG[2] WITH BLITZ. HE SEEMED TO BE SLEEPWALKING[3] HALF THE TIME.
IT WAS A BIT BORING[4], BUT AT LEAST LEFEVRE'S CUTE[5].
SABINA! HE'S SEVEN YEARS OLDER THAN YOU![6]
SORRY, MUM...
...
ARE YOU ENJOYING YOUR TIME[7] AS A BALL BOY[8], ALEX?
YES, THANKS, MR PLEASURE. IT'S—
RIDER! I NEED SOMEONE FOR STANDBY[9]. DO YOU MIND?[10]
NO, SIR. JUST GIVE ME A MINUTE.
ALEX, BEFORE YOU RUN OFF[11]...
WE'RE GOING ON HOLIDAY TO CORNWALL[12] NEXT WEEK. DO YOU WANT TO COME WITH US? WE COULD GO SURFING[13]!
ARE ... ARE YOU SURE?
WE'D LOVE TO HAVE YOU[14], ALEX. YOU CAN KEEP SABINA OUT OF TROUBLE.[15]
THAT WOULD BE GREAT[16]!
SORRY, I HAVE TO GO[17]. I'LL CALL YOU LATER!

A FAMILY HOLIDAY... I CAN'T IMAGINE WHAT THAT'S LIKE[1].
EVEN MY HOLIDAYS WITH UNCLE IAN DIDN'T REALLY FEEL LIKE A FAMILY THING[2].
AND SABINA'S PARENTS ARE REALLY NICE[3]. THEY SEEM LIKE A REALLY HAPPY FAMILY...
RIDER!
GET A MOVE ON[4], BOY, THE UMPIRE[5] HASN'T GOT ALL DAY!
YES, MR WALFOR! I'M COMING—
OH! SORRY!
THAT'LL TEACH ME TO DAYDREAM[6] WHILE I'M SUPPOSED TO BE WORKING... GET YOUR MIND ON[7] THE JOB, ALEX!

1. à quoi ça ressemble

2. un truc en famille

3. sympas

4. Dépêche-toi

5. l'arbitre

6. rêvasser

7. Concentre-toi sur

TWO DAYS LATER
WOW.
SWANKY PLACE![3]
CRAWFORD SAID THE BURGLAR[1] BROKE INTO THE MILLENNIUM BUILDING. MAYBE IF I TAKE A LOOK AROUND[2] IT MIGHT HELP...
IT'S THAT GUARD I BUMPED INTO[4] AGAIN...
WAIT A MINUTE, HE WAS USING THE PAYPHONE[5] IN THE CAFÉ A COUPLE OF DAYS AGO[6]. WHY BOTHER[7], IF HE'S GOT A MOBILE?
WHAT'S HE DOING, JUST STANDING THERE? HE KEEPS STARING AT[8]...
...OWEN BRYANT. ANOTHER WORLD-CLASS[9] PLAYER.
AND HE'S PLAYING[10] LEFEVRE THIS AFTERNOON, TOO.
HMMM.

1. le cambrioleur

2. si j'y jette un coup d'œil

3. C'est chic, comme endroit !

4. que j'ai heurté

5. téléphone public

6. il y a deux jours

7. Pourquoi s'embêter

8. Il n'arrête pas de fixer

9. de niveau international

10. il joue contre

NOW THE GUARD'S MAKING A CALL[1] AFTER ALL ... BUT HE HASN'T DIALLED ANYTHING[2] YET...
OH, MAYBE HE'S SENDING A TEXT[3]. HE ONLY PRESSED[4] ONE BUTTON[5], THOUGH[6]...
...AND NOW HE'S LEAVING AGAIN! WHAT ON EARTH IS GOING ON?![7]
CRAWFORD WAS RIGHT[8], SOMETHING HERE IS JUST PLAIN WRONG[9].
I NEED TO[10] TAKE A LOOK AT THAT PHONE.
OH! SORRY!

1. passe un coup de fil

2. composé aucun numéro

3. texto

4. appuyé sur

5. touche

6. pourtant

7. Mais qu'est-ce qui se passe ?!

8. avait raison

9. ne tourne pas rond du tout

10. Il faut que je

YOU AGAIN...!
YOU SHOULD WATCH WHERE YOU'RE GOING[1]!
I KNOW, SORRY!
MY MUM ALWAYS SAYS I'M IN MY OWN LITTLE WORLD[2]... HERE, LET ME GET THAT[3] FOR YOU.
WOW, IT WEIGHS ALMOST[4] NOTHING!
AND THERE'S NO NETWORK[5] LOGO, NOTHING ON THE SCREEN[6]...
HERE YOU GO[7]—
Snatch!
OH!
YOU'RE WELCOME.[8]
SO THE PHONE'S A FAKE[9]. BUT WHY?
AND WHAT DOES IT HAVE TO DO[10] WITH OWEN BRYANT?

1. où tu mets les pieds
2. que je vis dans mon petit monde à moi
3. le ramasser
4. il ne pèse presque
5. d'opérateur
6. l'écran
7. Tenez
8. Mais de rien.
9. faux
10. quel est le rapport

LIVE
BRYANT 6 6 4 2 0
LEFEVRE 4 7 6 5 15
...IN THE FOURTH[1] SET OF BRYANT VS[2] LEFEVRE, AND ONCE AGAIN[3] WE MAY HAVE AN EXTRAORDINARY UPSET ON OUR HANDS.
BRYANT STARTED THE DAY WELL[4], WITH A COMFORTABLE 6-4 VICTORY OVER THE FRENCHMAN[5] IN THE FIRST SET...
...BUT AFTER AN EXHAUSTING[6] SECOND SET THAT WENT 7-6 TO LEFEVRE, IT'S BEEN DOWNHILL[7] ALL THE WAY[8] FOR BRYANT. HE LOST THE THIRD[9] 6-4, AND THE FOURTH NOW STANDS AT[10] 5-2.
BUT LIKE BLITZ BEFORE HIM, BRYANT SEEMS COMPLETELY BAMBOOZLED[11] BY THE FRENCHMAN. HIS GAME HAS DISAPPEARED, AND SURELY THERE'S NO WAY[12]—
—NO, THERE ISN'T!
6 6
4 7
GAME, SET AND MATCH[13] TO LEFEVRE, AND THAT MAKES IT[14] 6-2.
ANOTHER SURPRISE KNOCKOUT[15]!

1. quatrième
2. [abréviation de « versus » signifiant « contre »]
3. une fois de plus
4. a bien commencé la journée
5. le Français
6. épuisant
7. Ça a été la dégringolade
8. tout le long
9. troisième
10. le score du quatrième est actuellement de
11. déboussolé
12. il n'y a sûrement aucune chance
13. Jeu, set et match
14. ce qui nous donne
15. K.O.

1. bizarre

2. plein de fois

3. là-bas

4. qu'il a simplement eu un jour sans

5. bien sonné

6. drogué

7. Tu es content d'aller en Cornouailles ?

8. qu'il louera

9. planche de surf

10. Ne quitte pas.

11. Chut.

12. ne permet pas de revenir

LATER
...TOTALLY WEIRD[1], SABINA. I'VE SEEN BRYANT PLAY LOADS OF TIMES[2] ON TV, BUT TODAY IT WAS LIKE A DIFFERENT PLAYER OUT THERE[3].
YEAH, I WATCHED IT. MAYBE HE WAS JUST HAVING AN OFF-DAY[4].
I DON'T KNOW, I SAW HIM AFTERWARDS AND HE LOOKED PRETTY ZONED OUT[5] ... ALMOST LIKE HE WAS ON DRUGS[6] OR SOMETHING.
ARE YOU LOOKING FORWARD TO CORNWALL?[7] DAD SAYS HE'LL HIRE[8] A SURFBOARD[9] FOR YOU IF YOU NEED ONE.
YEAH, THAT WOULD BE...
HOLD ON.[10]
ALEX? ALEX, ARE YOU THERE?
SHHH.[11] JUST A MINUTE...
STAFF ONLY
THAT DOOR DOESN'T LEAD BACK[12] TO THE COURTS... WHERE'S HE GOING?

SAB, I'VE GOT TO GO[1]. SORRY.
KLIK
ALEX! WHAT'S GOING—
HMPH. BOYS[2]!
THESE ARE THE SERVICE TUNNELS, UNDER THE MAIN GROUNDS[3].
RESTRICTED AREA
THIS IS THE "BUGGY ROUTE[4]". BUT HE'S A SECURITY GUARD ... HE SHOULDN'T BE IN HERE![5]
ACTUALLY[6], NEITHER SHOULD I...
NOW, WHERE DID HE...

1. je dois te laisser

2. ces garçons, alors

3. sous le site principal

4. passage pour les chariots

5. Il n'a rien à faire là !

6. En fait

1. perdu
2. une sorte de
3. sauf que
4. remplis de détritus
5. de provisions
6. quai de chargement
7. toujours pas
8. tout de même

A-HA.
OK, NOW I'M COMPLETELY LOST[1].
LOOKS LIKE SOME KIND OF[2] CAR PARK...
...EXCEPT[3] MOST CAR PARKS AREN'T FILLED WITH TRASH[4] AND FOOD SUPPLIES[5]. SO WHERE AM I?
Clap Clap Clap Clap
OF COURSE ... THIS IS THE LOADING BAY[6] RIGHT UNDER COURT NUMBER ONE!
DAN
I STILL DON'T[7] UNDERSTAND WHAT THAT GUARD'S DOING HERE, THOUGH[8].
DANGER

WHERE DID HE GO...?
..vrrrrrr
DANGER
Krash!
AAAH!!
HE KNEW I'D FOLLOW HIM[1]... IT'S A TRAP[2]!
Whoosh!
NNNH! HE'S FAST[3]...

1. que je le suivrais

2. piège

3. rapide

...REALLY FAST!
THNK!
UNH!
RAWLINGS REFRIGERATION
KRUMP
!
KLUNK!

Klank!
Rrip
Krash!
CAUTION
COMPRESSED AIR
COME HERE, LITTLE BOY. I WILL HAVE SUCH FUN[1] WITH YOU!
YEAH...
Pssshhh!
IT'LL BE A REAL GAS![2]
!
MY EYES!

1. Je vais bien m'amuser

2. [jeu de mots : Alex projette du gaz, mais sa phrase veut dire « on va bien se marrer ! »]

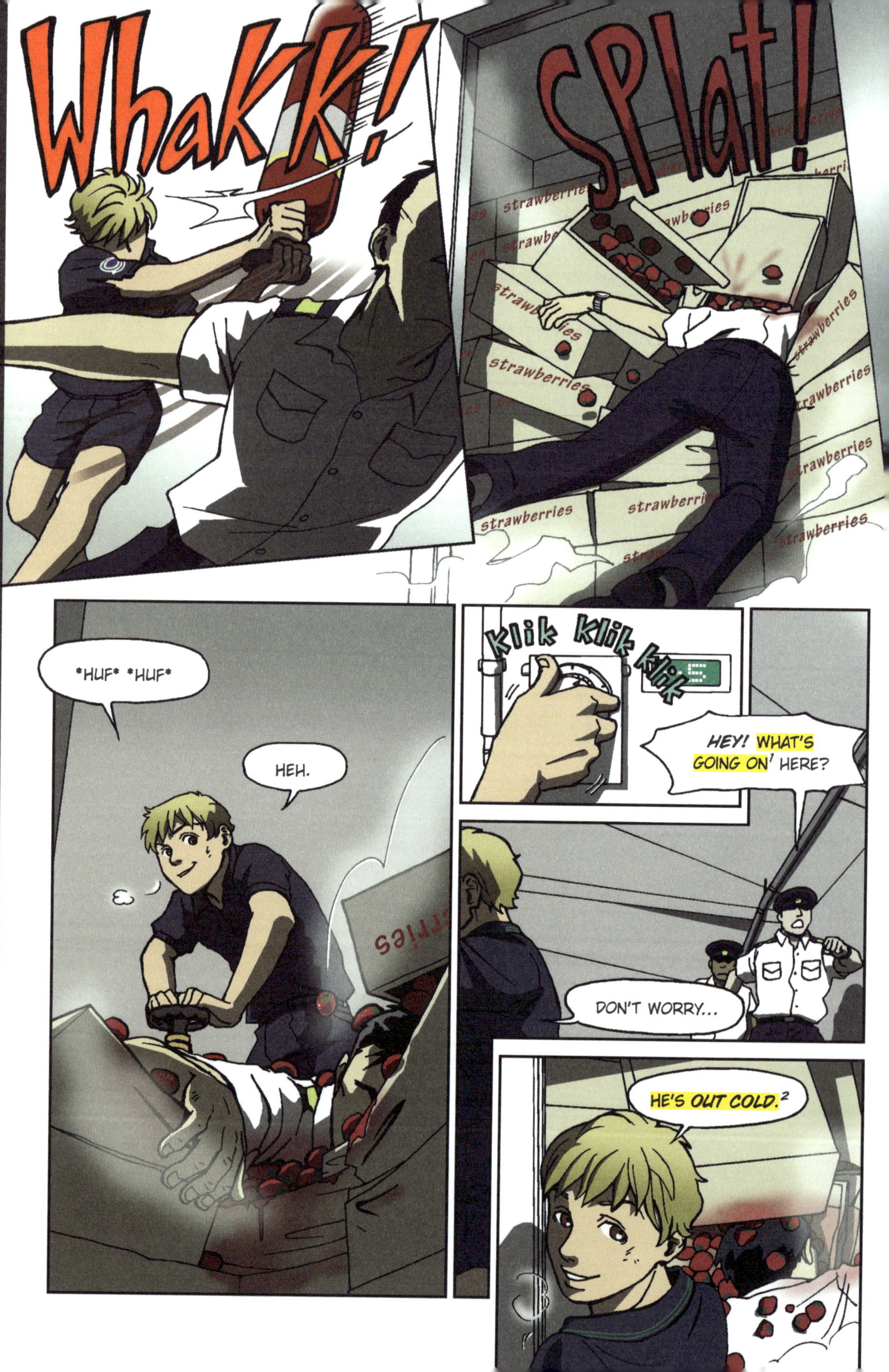
WhakK!
SPlat!
strawberries
HUF *HUF*
HEH.
Klik Klik Klik
HEY! WHAT'S GOING ON[1] HERE?
DON'T WORRY...
HE'S OUT COLD.[2]

1. Qu'est-ce qui se passe

2. Il dort. [jeu de mots : en effet, Alex l'a jeté dans une chambre froide (cold)]

THIS IS LIBRIUM. NASTY[2] LITTLE DRUG. A SPOONFUL[3] WILL KNOCK YOU OUT FOR HOURS, BUT A COUPLE OF DROPS[4] WILL JUST[5] CONFUSE YOU[6]. KNOCK YOU OFF BALANCE.[7]
IT'S BUILT INTO THE[1] FILTER, WITH A VALVE SYSTEM. VERY INGENIOUS.
SIR NORMAN, YOU REMEMBER I WAS WORRIED ABOUT THE BREAK-IN[8] WE HAD.
NOT THAT AGAIN, CRAWFORD ... THEY DIDN'T TAKE ANYTHING! WE SEARCHED THE ENTIRE CLUB!
BUT WE DIDN'T EXAMINE THE WATER DISPENSERS[9]. THEY WERE FIXING THEM UP![10] HERE, AND IN THE RESTAURANT ... PROBABLY ALL OVER[11] THE BUILDING.
ALL ACTIVATED BY REMOTE CONTROL[12].
THAT'S RIGHT. THE DISPENSER FUNCTIONS NORMALLY UNTIL IT RECEIVES[13] A RADIO SIGNAL FROM THAT FAKE PHONE.
THEN IT DISPENSES[14] A TINY AMOUNT[15] OF LIBRIUM INTO THE WATER. NOT ENOUGH TO SHOW UP[16] IN A BLOOD TEST[17], BUT ENOUGH TO RUIN[18] A PLAYER'S GAME.

1. intégré au

2. Une sale

3. Une cuillerée

4. deux ou trois gouttes

5. ne feront que

6. vous perturber

7. Vous désorienter.

8. cette intrusion

9. les distributeurs d'eau

10. Ils étaient en cours de réparation !

11. dans tout

12. télécommande

13. jusqu'à ce qu'il reçoive

14. il envoie

15. infime quantité

16. pour être détecté

17. prise de sang

18. pour gâcher

1. Des joueurs comme

2. goût

3. ne le remarquerait

4. gobelet

5. glacée

6. Dans quel but ?

7. tatouage

8. bras

9. Largement impliquée

10. les paris

11. une escroquerie liée aux paris

12. une cote

13. trois cents contre un

14. de ce qu'il se passait

15. adversaires

16. chaque match

17. durer jusqu'à

18. pari

19. au début

20. aurait rapporté

PLAYERS LIKE[1] BLITZ AND BRYANT.
IT'S TRANSPARENT, AND HAS VIRTUALLY NO TASTE[2]. NOBODY WOULD NOTICE IT[3] IN A CUP[4] OF ICED[5] WATER.
BUT I DON'T UNDERSTAND. WHAT WAS THE POINT?[6]
THE GUARD ISN'T TALKING, BUT THE TATTOO[7] ON HIS ARM[8] INDICATES THAT HE IS - OR WAS - A MEMBER OF THE BIG CIRCLE.
BIG CIRCLE IS A TRIAD, SIR - A CHINESE GANG. HEAVILY INVOLVED[9] IN DRUGS, VICE, PROSTITUTION ... AND GAMBLING[10]. I BELIEVE THIS WAS A GAMBLING SCAM[11].
THAT FRENCH PLAYER, LEFEVRE... HE STARTED THE TOURNAMENT WITH ODDS[12] OF THREE HUNDRED TO ONE AGAINST[13]!
EXACTLY. I'M SURE HE HAD NO IDEA WHAT WAS GOING ON[14], BUT IF HIS OPPONENTS[15] WERE DRUGGED BEFORE EACH GAME[16]... THIS COULD HAVE GONE ALL THE WAY[17] TO THE FINAL.
AND A HUNDRED THOUSAND POUNDS BET[18] ON LEFEVRE AT THE START[19] OF THE TOURNAMENT WOULD HAVE NETTED[20] THIRTY MILLION...!
WHAT ARE WE GOING TO DO?
NOTHING.

WHAT?
IF ANYONE FOUND OUT[1] IT WOULD BE A NATIONAL SCANDAL, AND DISASTROUS FOR OUR REPUTATION. WE'D HAVE TO RESTART[2] THE WHOLE TOURNAMENT ALL OVER AGAIN[3].
CAN THIS … BOY … BE TRUSTED NOT TO TALK?
RELAX. I WON'T TELL ANYONE.[4]
YOU DID A VERY GOOD JOB. STROKE OF LUCK[5], YOU SPOTTING[6] THIS CHAP[7] AND THEN FOLLOWING HIM.
YEAH, REALLY LUCKY.
I'M SURE WE CAN COME UP WITH[8] A SUITABLE REWARD[9] FOR HIM. COME ALONG[10], MY BOY.
NOT A WORD.[11] LET THEM THINK YOU'RE JUST A BALL BOY … ALTHOUGH[12] I THINK YOU'LL HAVE TO STOP WORKING AT THE TOURNAMENT.
THAT'S OK…
I'VE GOT A DATE[13] AT THE BEACH[14].

1. Si quelqu'un l'apprenait

2. recommencer

3. depuis le début

4. Je ne le dirai à personne.

5. Un vrai coup de chance

6. que tu aies repéré

7. type

8. qu'on peut trouver

9. une récompense appropriée

10. Viens avec moi

11. Ne dis pas un mot.

12. Bien que

13. un rendez-vous

14. plage

1. agité

2. taille

3. vagues

4. Ça fait trois jours qu'on est ici

5. [ou Cribbar, du nom d'un récif, en Cornouailles, qui crée à une certaine époque de l'année des vagues d'environ 9 m, connues des passionnés de surf]

6. géante

7. depuis des années

8. Peut-être bien

9. je ne me le pardonnerai jamais

10. laisse passer

11. de la surfer

12. que j'évalue le bon moment

IT'S TOO ROUGH[1]! LOOK AT THE SIZE[2] OF THOSE WAVES[3]!
FISTRAL BEACH, CORNWALL
TYPICAL BRITISH SUMMER! WE'VE BEEN HERE THREE DAYS[4], AND NOT ONE DAY OF DECENT WATER!
IT'S THE CRIBBER[5]!
ALEX, WHAT ARE YOU DOING?
THE CRIBBER'S A GIANT[6] WAVE! IT HASN'T COME TO ENGLAND FOR YEARS[7]!
BUT IT'S DANGEROUS!
IT MIGHT BE[8]... BUT I'LL NEVER FORGIVE MYSELF[9] IF I MISS[10] THE CHANCE TO RIDE IT[11]!
HERE IT COMES! GOT TO TIME IT[12]...

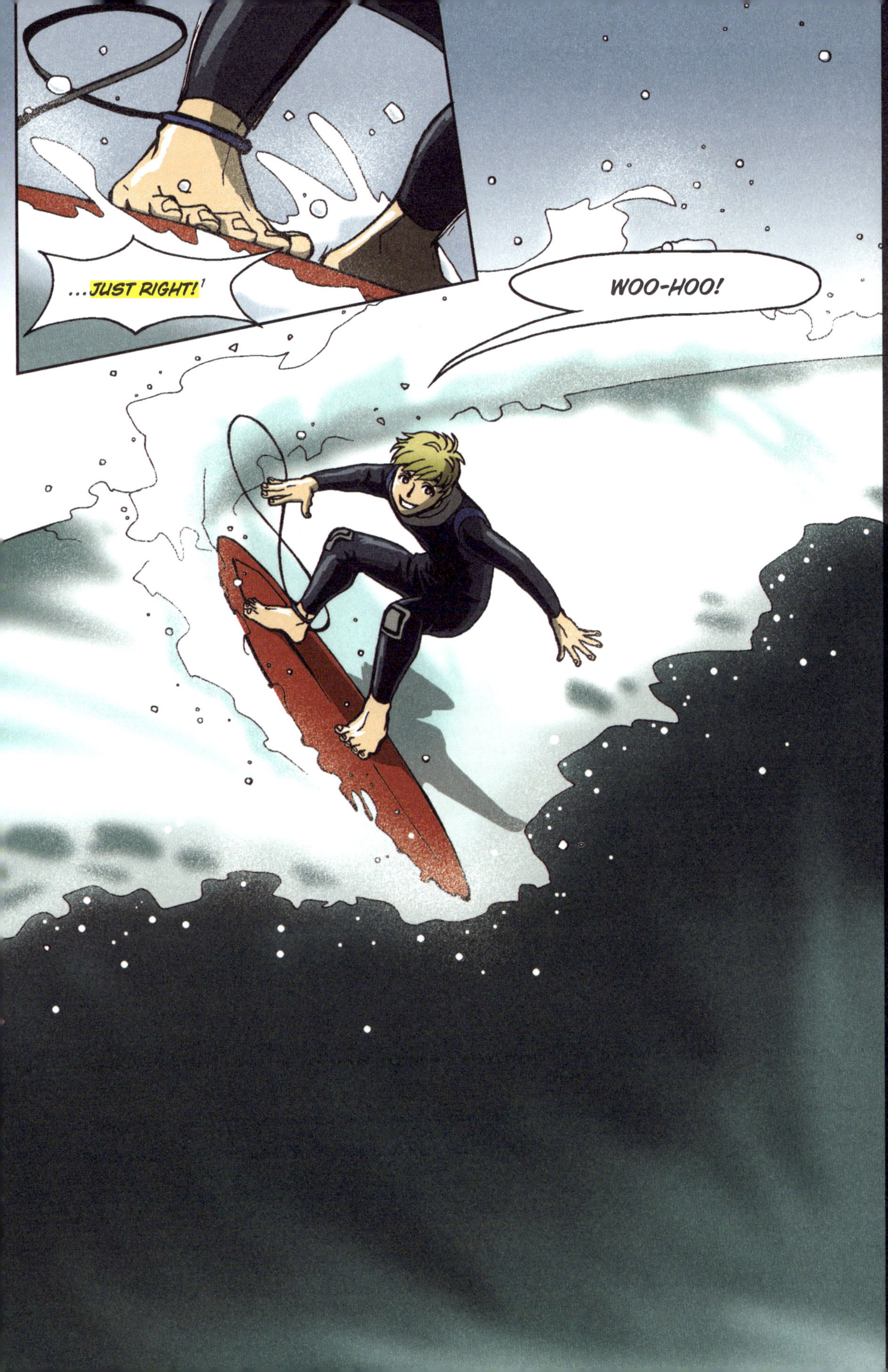
...JUST RIGHT![1]
WOO-HOO!

1. Parfait !

UH-OH...
SPLASH!
DID YOU SEE THAT? IT WAS AWESOME[1]! WELL, APART FROM FALLING IN[2] AT THE END, BUT...
ALEX...
...THERE'S SOMEONE TO SEE YOU.[3]
HELLO, ALEX. SORRY TO INTERRUPT[4] YOUR HOLIDAY.
YOU AGAIN[5], MR CRAWFORD! HOW DID YOU EVEN FIND ME?
WE HAVE WAYS[6], ALEX, YOU KNOW THAT.
I'M AFRAID[7] MR BLUNT IS ON THE WARPATH[8]. HE NEEDS TO SEE YOU TODAY.

1. génial

2. sauf lorsque je suis tombé

3. quelqu'un veut te voir.

4. d'interrompre

5. Encore vous

6. Nous disposons de moyens

7. J'ai bien peur que

8. sur le sentier de la guerre

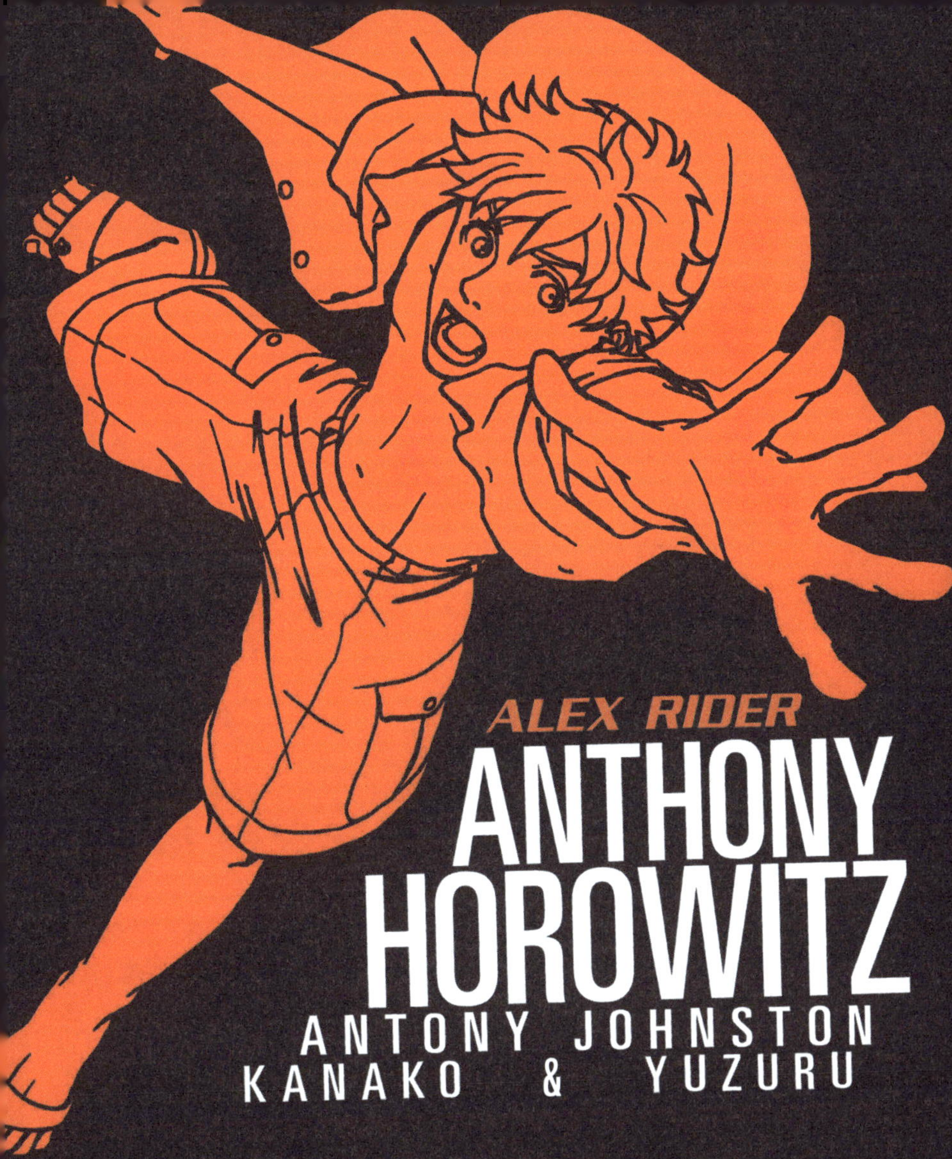

ALEX RIDER

ANTHONY HOROWITZ

ANTONY JOHNSTON

KANAKO & YUZURU

HARRAP'S

GRAPHIC NOVELS

SKELETON KEY

1. n'avait pas le droit

2. dans cette affaire

3. aurais pu te faire tuer

4. Je n'aime pas que

5. des risques inutiles

6. l'un de

7. sans devoir en rajouter

8. S'attaquer à

9. tout seul

10. énorme

11. Le Grand Cercle

12. relativement récente

13. l'une des plus

14. Ils n'apprécient guère

15. se mêlent de

16. la leçon

17. Je m'en souviendrai.

18. de ce dans quoi tu t'es mis

LIVERPOOL STREET, LONDON
CRAWFORD HAD NO RIGHT[1] TO INVOLVE YOU IN THIS BUSINESS[2].
YOU COULD HAVE GOT YOURSELF KILLED[3]. I DON'T LIKE[4] MY AGENTS TAKING UNNECESSARY RISKS[5].
I'M NOT ONE OF[6] YOUR AGENTS.
THERE'S ENOUGH DANGER IN OFFICIAL MISSIONS WITHOUT ADDING TO IT[7]. TAKING ON[8] A TRIAD SINGLE-HANDED[9]!
IT WAS JUST ONE MAN.
BUT THAT MAN IS PART OF A HUGE[10] ORGANIZATION. BIG CIRCLE[11] IS A RELATIVELY NEW[12] TRIAD, BUT IT'S ALSO ONE OF THE MOST[13] VIOLENT.
THEY DON'T TAKE KINDLY TO[14] PEOPLE INTERFERING WITH[15] THEIR BUSINESS.
THANKS FOR THE LECTURE[16]. I'LL BEAR IT IN MIND.[17]
SIT DOWN, ALEX. YOU HAVE NO IDEA WHAT YOU'VE GOT YOURSELF INTO[18].

THE TRIAD OPERATES UNDER A PRINCIPLE[1] OF GUAN-SHI - A SYSTEM OF MUTUAL RESPECT. IT'S WHAT GIVES THE TRIAD ITS POWER[2].
IT MEANS THAT IF YOU HURT[3] ONE OF THEM, YOU HURT THEM ALL.
SO IF ONE OF THEM BECOMES[4] YOUR ENEMY, THEY ALL DO[5]. EVERY OTHER[6] MEMBER. THERE'S ALREADY A PRICE ON YOUR HEAD.[7]
HOW MANY[8] "OTHER MEMBERS" ARE THERE...?
NINETEEN THOUSAND, AT THE LAST COUNT[9].
EVERY MINUTE YOU STAY IN ENGLAND, YOU'RE IN DANGER. WE HAVE SOME INFLUENCE[10] IN THE TRIADS, BUT IT WILL TAKE TIME TO CALL THEM OFF[11].
TIME YOU DON'T HAVE.[12]
I'M SUPPOSED TO BE[13] IN CORNWALL. ON HOLIDAY...
OUT OF THE QUESTION. YOU MAY ALREADY HAVE BEEN SPOTTED[14] BEFORE WE BROUGHT YOU IN[15].

1. fonctionne selon un principe

2. sa puissance

3. si tu fais du mal à

4. devient

5. ils le deviennent tous

6. Tous les autres

7. Ta tête est déjà mise à prix.

8. Combien de

9. au dernier recensement

10. Nous avons une certaine influence

11. pour les neutraliser

12. Ce temps, tu n'en disposes pas.

13. Je suis censé être

14. repéré

15. qu'on t'amène ici

THE FACT IS[1], ALEX, YOU CAN'T GO HOME[2]. YOU CAN'T GO TO SCHOOL. YOU CAN'T GO ANYWHERE[3] ON YOUR OWN[4].
WE'VE ALREADY ARRANGED FOR JACK STARBRIGHT TO BE SENT OUT OF LONDON. WE CAN'T TAKE ANY CHANCES.[5]
SO WHAT AM I MEANT TO DO?[6]
WELL...
BY COINCIDENCE[7], WE HAD A REQUEST[8] FOR YOUR SERVICES A FEW DAYS AGO[9].
THE AMERICAN CIA NEEDS A YOUNG PERSON FOR AN OPERATION THEY'RE MOUNTING[10].
YOU'VE ALWAYS TOLD ME TO KEEP EVERYTHING SECRET, BUT ALL THIS TIME YOU'VE BEEN BRAGGING ABOUT ME[11]?!
ABSOLUTELY NOT.
BUT THINGS HAVE A WAY OF[12]...
LEAKING[13]...
IN OUR LINE OF WORK[14].

1. Le fait est
2. rentrer chez toi
3. nulle part
4. tout seul
5. Nous ne pouvons prendre aucun risque.
6. Et moi, je suis censé faire quoi, alors ?
7. Par pure coïncidence
8. une demande
9. il y a quelques jours
10. qu'ils sont en train de monter
11. vous vous vantiez de mon existence
12. arrivent à
13. filtrer
14. métier

WE TOLD THEM[1] YOU WEREN'T INTERESTED. A SCHOOLBOY, NOT A SPY, THAT'S WHAT YOU SAID[2].
BUT THIS TRIAD BUSINESS[3] CHANGES EVERYTHING.
YOU HAVE TO DISAPPEAR, ALEX. YOU HAVE TO GO SOMEWHERE THE TRIAD WON'T EVEN THINK OF LOOKING FOR YOU.
SO YOU WANT TO SEND ME[4] TO AMERICA?
CUBA, ACTUALLY[5]. OR RATHER[6], AN ISLAND[7] JUST A FEW MILES SOUTH[8].
CAYO ESQUELETO, IT'S CALLED, WHICH IS SPANISH FOR[9]...
SKELETON KEY[10].
CORRECT. DESPITE ITS NAME[11], IT'S NOT DANGEROUS AT ALL.
IT'S A TOURIST RESORT[12], WITH LUXURY[13] HOTELS, DIVING[14], SAILING[15] AND SO ON.
THE CIA IS INTERESTED IN[16] THIS MAN. GENERAL ALEXEI SAROV.
SAROV HAS A HUGE HOUSE ON THE NORTHERN TIP[17] OF THE ISLAND. A PALACE, ALMOST[18].
SAROV WAS A COMMANDER[19] IN THE RUSSIAN ARMY, BACK WHEN[20] THE RUSSIANS WERE OUR ENEMIES, PART OF THE SOVIET UNION[21].
THAT ENDED[22] IN 1989, WHEN THE BERLIN WALL CAME DOWN[23].

1. On leur a bien dit
2. tu l'as dit toi-même
3. cette histoire de triade
4. m'envoyer
5. en réalité
6. Ou plutôt
7. île
8. à quelques kilomètres au sud
9. en espagnol cela veut dire
10. l'île du squelette
11. malgré son nom
12. station balnéaire
13. de luxe
14. de la plongée
15. de la voile
16. s'intéresse à
17. extrémité nord
18. quasiment
19. commandant
20. à l'époque où
21. [l'Union soviétique ou l'Union des républiques socialistes soviétiques (URSS)]
22. Tout cela s'est terminé
23. à la chute du mur de Berlin

1. l'ancienne Russie
2. Général à trente-huit ans
3. ont envahi
4. Il a combattu là-bas
5. promu aux fonctions de
6. comman-dant en second
7. Armée rouge
8. Son propre fils
9. tué
10. s'est achevée
11. s'est effondré
12. haïssait
13. baskets
14. à tous les coins de rue
15. demeure
16. pays
17. depuis ce temps-là
18. en se faisant toujours appeler
19. dans deux semaines
20. a l'intention de lui rendre visite
21. ayant grandi
22. a derrière la tête
23. une équipe infiltrée

SAROV WAS A HERO OF THE OLD RUSSIA[1]. A GENERAL AT JUST THIRTY-EIGHT[2], THE SAME YEAR THE RUSSIANS INVADED[3] AFGHANISTAN.
HE FOUGHT THERE[4] FOR TEN YEARS, RISING TO BECOME[5] SECOND IN COMMAND[6] OF THE ENTIRE RED ARMY[7]. HIS OWN SON[8] WAS KILLED[9] THERE.
THE WAR IN AFGHANISTAN ENDED[10] THE SAME YEAR COMMUNISM COLLAPSED[11].
SAROV HATED[12] THE NEW RUSSIA, WITH ITS JEANS, NIKE TRAINERS[13] AND MCDONALD'S ON EVERY CORNER[14].
SO HE LEFT.
HE WENT TO SKELETON KEY BECAUSE CUBA REMAINS[15] A COMMUNIST COUNTRY[16]. HE'S BEEN THERE EVER SINCE[17], STILL CALLING HIMSELF[18] GENERAL.
AND IN TWO WEEKS' TIME[19], THE RUSSIAN PRESIDENT IS PLANNING TO VISIT HIM[20] THERE.
THEY'RE OLD FRIENDS, GROWING UP[21] IN THE SAME PART OF MOSCOW. BUT THE CIA IS WORRIED.
THEY WANT TO KNOW WHAT SAROV IS UP TO[22]. WHY IS OLD RUSSIA MEETING NEW RUSSIA? WHAT'S GOING ON?
IT'S A SIMPLE SURVEILLANCE OPERATION. THEY WANT AN UNDERCOVER TEAM[23] TO GO IN AND TAKE A LOOK AROUND BEFORE THE PRESIDENT ARRIVES.
BUT WHY DO THEY NEED ME?

GETTING IN AND OUT[1] OF ANY[2] COMMUNIST COUNTRY IS VERY DIFFICULT. EVERY AEROPLANE IS WATCHED[3], EVERY PASSENGER CHECKED[4].
THEY'RE ALWAYS ON THE LOOKOUT[5] FOR AMERICAN SPIES. ANYONE EVEN SLIGHTLY[6] SUSPECT IS TURNED AWAY[7].
A SINGLE MAN[8] WOULD BE SUSPICIOUS. A MAN AND A WOMAN MIGHT BE[9] A TEAM. BUT...
BUT A FAMILY IS JUST ON HOLIDAY[10].
EXACTLY.
WHY NOT USE[11] AN AMERICAN BOY?
WELL[12], YOU SEE...
THE AMERICANS WOULD NEVER USE[13] ONE OF THEIR OWN[14] YOUNG PEOPLE FOR THIS SORT OF THING. THEY HAVE DIFFERENT RULES TO US[15].
YOU MEAN THEY'RE WORRIED HE MIGHT GET KILLED[16].
WE WOULDN'T ASK YOU EITHER, ALEX, BUT YOU HAVE TO LEAVE[17] THE COUNTRY, AND THE MISSION'S PERFECTLY SAFE[18].
THINK OF IT LIKE A PAID HOLIDAY[19]. TWO WEEKS IN THE SUN[20].
I DON'T HAVE MUCH CHOICE[21], DO I[22]?
SO WHEN DO YOU WANT ME TO LEAVE[23]?
THIS AFTERNOON. YOUR FLIGHT[24] IS ALREADY BOOKED[25].
BUT FIRST, YOU SHOULD GO AND SEE[26] SMITHERS.

1. Entrer et sortir
2. n'importe quel
3. surveillé
4. contrôlé
5. à l'affût
6. légèrement
7. renvoyé
8. Un homme seul
9. pourraient bien être
10. est simplement en vacances
11. ne pas avoir recours à
12. Eh bien
13. n'emploieraient jamais
14. leurs propres
15. des règles différentes des nôtres
16. qu'il se fasse tuer
17. tu dois quitter
18. sûre
19. vacances tous frais payés
20. soleil
21. vraiment le choix
22. n'est-ce pas
23. que je parte
24. vol
25. réservé
26. aller voir

1. Quel bonheur
2. Entre
3. bureau
4. Je m'attendais à
5. jouets
6. des scientifiques
7. des trucs
8. est en bas
9. laboratoire
10. que tu pars
11. tu as l'air en forme
12. charpente osseuse
13. appareil à rayons X
14. une arme à feu
15. de bons agents
16. jamais leur faire confiance
17. Génial.

MY DEAR BOY! HOW DELIGHTFUL[1] TO SEE YOU.
COME IN[2], COME IN!
HELLO, MR SMITHERS. IS THIS REALLY YOUR OFFICE[3]?
I WAS EXPECTING[4] MORE ... EXPLODING TOYS[5], AND SCIENTISTS[6], AND STUFF[7].
NO, ALL THAT SORT OF THING IS DOWN[8] IN THE LAB[9]. PLEASE, DO SIT DOWN.
DOOR!
klik
MR BLUNT TELLS ME YOU'RE OFF[10] TO JOIN OUR FRIENDS IN THE CIA.
MY, YOU'RE LOOKING WELL[11]. GOOD BONE STRUCTURE[12]!
Whrrrrr
...WHAT?
A SIMPLE X-RAY DEVICE[13]. USEFUL IF ANYONE IS WEARING A GUN[14].
I ... SEE.
NOW, THE AMERICANS ARE FINE OPERATORS[15]. EXCEPT OF COURSE THAT YOU CAN NEVER TRUST THEM[16], AND THEY HAVE NO SENSE OF HUMOUR.
GREAT.[17]

I'M TOLD[1] YOU NEED SOMETHING TO KEEP IN TOUCH[2] WITH US.
YEAH. A SECRET TRANSMITTER[3].
WHY DOES IT HAVE TO BE SECRET?
A MOBILE[4]? BUT I'VE ALREADY GOT ONE.
NOT LIKE THIS!
A DIRECT LINK[5] WITH THIS OFFICE, EVEN FROM AMERICA. IT WORKS UNDERWATER. FINGERPRINT SENSITIVE PADS[6], SO ONLY YOU CAN USE IT.
THIS IS THE MODEL FIVE. WE ALSO HAVE A MODEL SEVEN, WHICH EXPLODES UNLESS YOU DIAL[7] HOLDING IT[8] UPSIDE DOWN[9]...
CAN'T I HAVE THAT ONE?
SORRY, MR BLUNT HAS FORBIDDEN IT[10].
HOWEVER[11]...
DIAL 999 AND THE AERIAL[12] SHOOTS OUT[13] LIKE A NEEDLE[14]. DRUGGED, OF COURSE. IT'S GOT A TWENTY-METRE RANGE[15]. IT'LL KNOCK ANYONE OUT.
COOL. ANYTHING ELSE?[16]
I WAS TOLD YOU WEREN'T TO HAVE[17] ANY WEAPONS. HOWEVER...
COULD YOU BRING THEM UP, PLEASE, MISS PICKERING?

1. On m'a dit

2. pour rester en contact

3. émetteur

4. téléphone portable

5. liaison directe

6. Les touches reconnaissent les empreintes digitales

7. sauf si tu composes le numéro

8. en le tenant

9. à l'envers

10. me l'a interdit

11. Cependant

12. l'antenne

13. s'éjecte

14. aiguille

15. portée de vingt mètres

16. Autre chose ?

17. que tu ne devais pas avoir

I'M BENDING THE RULES[1] DOING THIS, BUT THERE ARE A COUPLE OF THINGS I'VE BEEN DEVELOPING FOR YOU, AND I DON'T SEE WHY YOU SHOULDN'T TAKE THEM NOW.
Whirrrrr
HERE ARE THE ITEMS[2] YOU REQUESTED, MR SMITHERS.
THANK YOU, MISS PICKERING. TAKE THE LIFT OUT[3], PLEASE.
BUBBLEGUM?[4]
CHEW FOR[5] THIRTY SECONDS AND THE COMPOUND[6] REACTS WITH YOUR SALIVA[7], MAKING IT EXPAND. AS IT EXPANDS, IT'LL SHATTER[8] JUST ABOUT[9] ANYTHING.
I CALL IT BUBBLE 0-7[10]! HA!
PUT IT IN A LOCK[11], FOR EXAMPLE, AND IT'LL CRACK OPEN[12]. OR THE BARREL[13] OF A GUN.
NOW, THIS ONE IS CALLED THE STRIKER[14], AND I'M SURE YOU WON'T NEED IT. BUT HERE YOU GO.
MICHAEL OWEN?
BUT I SUPPORT[15] CHELSEA.
OH. WELL, IT'S ONLY A PROTOTYPE, WE CAN DO A DIFFERENT PLAYER[16] NEXT TIME. THE IMPORTANT THING IS THE HEAD[17].

1. J'enfreins le règlement
2. les objets
3. Prenez l'ascenseur pour sortir
4. Des chewing-gums ?
5. Mâche-le pendant
6. mélange
7. ta salive
8. cela détruira
9. à peu près
10. [allusion à l'agent 007, James Bond]
11. serrure
12. elle se fendra en deux
13. canon
14. l'attaquant
15. je suis supporter de
16. joueur
17. tête

NOW REMEMBER THIS, ALEX. TWIST[1] THE HEAD TWICE[2] CLOCKWISE[3], THEN ONCE[4] ANTICLOCKWISE[5], TO ARM[6] THE DEVICE[7].
IT EXPLODES?
ONLY A STUN BLAST[8]. FLASHBANG[9], AS THEY SAY. TEN SECOND FUSE.[10] IT WON'T KILL, BUT IT WILL INCAPACITATE THE OPPOSITION[11] FOR A COUPLE OF MINUTES, GIVING YOU A CHANCE TO GET AWAY.
THANKS, MR SMITHERS. I FEEL BETTER[12] NOT GOING IN EMPTY-HANDED[13].
WRRRR...
GOOD LUCK, ALEX. I HOPE YOU GET ON ALL RIGHT[14] WITH THE CIA. THEY'RE NOT LIKE US AT ALL, YOU KNOW. HEAVEN KNOWS[15] WHAT THEY'LL MAKE OF YOU!
YOU CAN TAKE MY PRIVATE LIFT, IF YOU'RE GOING DOWNSTAIRS[16].
UH...
NO, THANKS. I'LL TAKE THE STAIRS[17].
WHATEVER YOU SAY.[18] JUST LOOK AFTER YOURSELF[19].
AND DON'T SWALLOW[20] THE GUM!

1. Fais tourner

2. deux fois

3. dans le sens des aiguilles d'une montre

4. une fois

5. dans le sens contraire des aiguilles d'une montre

6. armer

7. dispositif

8. explosion incapacitante

9. [nom d'une grenade qui émet un flash aveuglant]

10. Détonateur réglé à dix secondes.

11. l'adversaire

12. Ça me rassure

13. les mains vides

14. que tu t'entendras bien

15. Dieu seul sait

16. si tu descends

17. l'escalier

18. Comme tu veux.

19. fais attention à toi

20. n'avale pas

1. marchons un peu

2. Je dois vous rendre justice, à vous les rosbifs.

3. de mettre

4. un micro

5. collier

6. du beau travail

7. le choix

8. fatigué

9. allons-y

10. je te présente

11. Ils joueront le rôle de

MIAMI, USA
YOU MUST BE RIDER. I'M JOE BYRNE.
COME ON, LET'S TAKE A WALK[1].
CENTURION INTERNATIONAL ADVERTIZING
I HAVE TO HAND IT TO YOU BRITS.[2] WE'VE USED ANIMALS - TRIED TO PUT[3] A CAT INTO THE KOREAN EMBASSY WITH A BUG[4] ON ITS COLLAR[5]. UNFORTUNATELY, THEY ATE IT...
MY COUNTRY DIDN'T GIVE ME MUCH CHOICE[7].
BUT WE'VE NEVER USED A KID BEFORE. YOU'VE DONE GREAT WORK[6] FOR YOUR COUNTRY.
ANYWAY, YOU MUST BE TIRED[8], SO LET'S MOVE ON[9].
ALEX, MEET[10] SPECIAL AGENTS TOM TURNER AND BELINDA TROY. THEY'LL BE PLAYING[11] YOUR PARENTS DURING THIS OPERATION.

NICE TO MEET YOU[1], ALEX.
HOW WAS THE FLIGHT? IT MUST HAVE BEEN SCARY[2], TRAVELLING ON YOUR OWN[3].
I HAD TO CLOSE MY EYES[4] DURING TAKE-OFF[5], BUT I STOPPED TREMBLING WHEN WE GOT TO THIRTY-FIVE THOUSAND FEET[6].
YOU'RE SCARED OF FLYING?![7]
THIS IS CRAZY[8]! YOU'RE PUTTING THIS KID INTO A CIA OPERATION AND HE'S—
BELINDA! TOM! CALM DOWN! ALEX WAS JOKING[9].
HE'S BRITISH, REMEMBER? DIFFERENT SENSE OF HUMOUR.[10]
WELL, I DIDN'T FIND IT FUNNY[11]. THIS WHOLE IDEA IS[12] CRAZY.
YOU SAY THIS BOY HAS A REPUTATION, BUT HE'S STILL A MINOR[13]! AND WHAT ABOUT THAT ACCENT OF HIS? NO-ONE WILL BELIEVE[14] HE'S AMERICAN!
DAMMIT[15], WE'VE BEEN THROUGH THIS[16]... YOU KNOW HOW TOUGH[17] THEIR SECURITY IS. WITH THE RUSSIAN PRESIDENT ON HIS WAY[18], IT'LL BE WORSE THAN EVER[19].
WITHOUT A KID[20] YOU WON'T EVEN MAKE IT OUT[21] THE OTHER SIDE[22] OF SANTIAGO[23] AIRPORT!

1. Enchanté
2. effrayant
3. de voyager tout seul
4. fermer les yeux
5. le décollage
6. [10 668 m]
7. Tu as peur en avion ?!
8. dingue
9. plaisante
10. Ils n'ont pas le même sens de l'humour.
11. drôle
12. Cette idée est totalement
13. il est encore mineur
14. Personne ne croira
15. Bon sang
16. on en a déjà parlé
17. stricte
18. en chemin
19. pire que jamais
20. Sans gosse
21. n'atteindrez même pas
22. côté
23. [ville portuaire située au sud-est de l'île de Cuba et capitale de la province de Santiago de Cuba]

1. le former pour qu'il atteigne

2. niveau

3. N'y pense même pas

4. de faux papiers d'identité

5. prénoms

6. Et si

7. Tout est verrouillé

8. tout sera confirmé

9. [abréviation de Los Angeles]

10. qu'ils vous connaissent depuis toujours

11. la Maison dorée

12. qui est l'endroit où

13. habite

14. Une fois que

15. sur

16. rester à l'écart

17. profiter de

18. vacances

SO FIND AN AMERICAN KID.
AND TRAIN HIM UP TO[1] ALEX'S LEVEL[2] IN TWO DAYS? FORGET IT[3], TOM. NOW LET ME TELL YOU HOW IT'S GOING TO WORK.
YOU'LL ALL NEED FAKE IDs[4]. IT'LL BE EASIER TO KEEP YOUR FIRST NAMES[5], SO IT'S ALEX GARDINER TRAVELLING WITH HIS PARENTS, TOM AND BELINDA GARDINER.
WHAT IF[6] SOMEONE CHECKS UP ON US?
USA
GARDINER
ALEX
CALIFORNIA, U.S.A.
IT'S ALL BEEN BACKSTOPPED[7], SO EVERYTHING WILL CHECK OUT[8]. WE HAVE PEOPLE UP IN LA[9] WHO'LL SAY THEY'VE KNOWN YOU ALL YOUR LIFE[10].
NOW, TURNER AND TROY NEED TO GET INTO CASA DE ORO - THAT'S "GOLDEN HOUSE[11]" - WHICH IS WHERE[12] GENERAL SAROV LIVES[13].
YOU WANT TO KNOW WHAT HE'S DOING?
RIGHT. ONCE[14] YOU'VE HELPED GET TURNER AND TROY ONTO[15] THE ISLAND, YOU CAN KEEP OUT OF THEIR WAY[16]. JUST STAY IN THE HOTEL AND ENJOY[17] YOUR VACATION[18].

YOU HAVE TWO DAYS TILL YOU LEAVE[1], AND I WANT YOU TO SPEND[2] ALL OF THAT TIME TOGETHER[3].
STARTING TOMORROW[4], THINK LIKE A FAMILY. BECAUSE THAT'S WHAT YOU'VE GOT TO BE.
SIR, I HAVE A MEETING[5] WITH THE SALESMAN[6] AT NOON[7] TOMORROW! I DON'T THINK HE'S EXPECTING MY WIFE AND SON TO JOIN US[8].
AND I'M SUPPOSED TO BE HIS BACKUP[9].
WELL ... THE SALESMAN IS ALWAYS ON THE WATER, RIGHT? SO TOM, YOU GO ONTO THE[10] BOAT WHILE ALEX AND BELINDA STAY ON DRY LAND[11].
WE'LL PICK YOU UP[12] FROM YOUR HOTEL AT TEN-THIRTY[13], ALEX. DON'T BE LATE[14].
YAWN[15]
OK.
I WANT TO SAY AGAIN HOW GRATEFUL I AM[16] THAT YOU AGREED[17] TO HELP US OUT.
I'M SURE EVERYTHING WILL WORK OUT FINE[18].
YEAH[19], RIGHT.

1. avant de partir

2. que vous passiez

3. ensemble

4. Dès demain

5. une réunion

6. vendeur

7. midi

8. se joignent à nous

9. renfort

10. montes à bord du

11. sur la terre ferme

12. On viendra te chercher

13. dix heures trente

14. en retard

15. [il bâille]

16. le dire encore à quel point je te suis reconnaissant

17. d'avoir accepté

18. se passera bien

19. Ouais

1. Entrez.
2. réussi à récupérer
3. billets
4. marécage
5. blanchi
6. encaissé
7. Tout se passe comme prévu.
8. Achevée.
9. compter sur toi
10. combien il attend impatiemment
11. inoubliables
12. pièces
13. sont prêtes
14. il reste encore

Knock Knock
ENTER.[1]
CASA DE ORO, CAYO ESQUELETO
GOOD MORNING, CONRAD. I HOPE WE'VE MANAGED TO RECOVER[2] THE REST OF THE BANKNOTES[3] FROM THE SWAMP[4].
YESH.
THE MONEY MUST BE LAUNDERED[5], OF COURSE, BEFORE IT CAN BE PAID INTO MY ACCOUNT[6].
EVERYTHING IS PROCEEDING ACCORDING TO PLAN.[7] THE CONSTRUCTION OF THE BOMB...?
KHOMPLETE.[8]
I KNEW I COULD RELY ON YOU[9]. THE PRESIDENT ARRIVES IN FIVE DAYS.
I HAD AN EMAIL FROM HIM TODAY TO SAY HOW MUCH HE'S LOOKING FORWARD TO[10] HIS HOLIDAY.
IT WILL, OF COURSE, BE ONE HE WILL NEVER FORGET[11].
THE ROOMS[12] AND CAMERAS ARE READY[13]?
YESH.
GOOD. BUT THERE STILL REMAINS[14] THE QUESTION OF THE URANIUM.

I ALWAYS KNEW THE PURCHASE AND DELIVERY[1] OF NUCLEAR MATERIAL WOULD BE DANGEROUS. THE MEN IN THE AIRCRAFT[2] THREATENED ME[3], AND PAID THE PRICE.
BUT, OF COURSE, THEY WERE WORKING FOR A THIRD PARTY[4].
BY NOW[5], THE SALESMAN WILL HAVE GUESSED[6] WHAT HAPPENED TO HIS MESSENGERS. WHEN NO FURTHER PAYMENT[7] ARRIVES FROM ME, HE MAY CARRY OUT HIS THREAT[8] TO ALERT THE AUTHORITIES.
UNLIKELY[9], BUT A RISK I CANNOT AFFORD TO TAKE[10].
IN LESS THAN TWO WEEKS, THE BOMB WILL BE DETONATED[11] AND THE WORLD WILL TAKE ON THE SHAPE[12] I HAVE DECIDED TO GIVE IT. WE CANNOT TAKE ANY CHANCES[13].
CONRAD, YOU MUST GO TO[14] MIAMI.
WHERR IZH HE?
HE OPERATES OUT OF A BOAT[15] CALLED MAYFAIR LADY, USUALLY MOORED[16] AT THE BAYSIDE MARKETPLACE. THE SALESMAN FEELS SAFER[17] ON THE WATER.
PERSONALLY, I WILL FEEL SAFER WHEN HE IS UNDERNEATH IT[18].
YESH, GENERAHL.

1. que l'achat et la livraison

2. avion

3. m'ont menacé

4. une tierce personne

5. À cette heure-ci

6. aura deviné

7. paiement supplémentaire

8. mettre sa menace à exécution

9. C'est peu probable

10. me permettre de prendre

11. explosera

12. prendra la forme

13. aucun risque

14. tu dois te rendre à

15. Il dirige ses affaires depuis un bateau

16. amarré

17. se sent plus en sécurité

18. il sera tout au fond

1. Tu as bien dormi
2. Je me suis réveillé des heures
3. commander
4. complet
5. de campagne
6. confiture
7. Il veut dire
8. Si tu fais ce genre de faux-pas
9. en prison
10. en un clin d'œil
11. je n'ai pas réfléchi
12. Comment va
13. C'est Mrs Beach qui s'en occupe
14. voisine

BAYSIDE MARKETPLACE, MIAMI
SLEEP WELL[1], ALEX?
NOT REALLY. I WAS AWAKE HOURS[2] BEFORE YOU CAME TO PICK ME UP.
ARE YOU READY TO ORDER[3] BREAKFAST?
I'LL JUST HAVE ORANGE JUICE AND TOAST.
WHOLEMEAL[4] OR GRANARY[5]?
GRANARY, WITH BUTTER AND JAM[6]...
HAHA! HE MEANS[7] JELLY!
NO AMERICAN KID ASKS FOR "JAM".
YOU SLIP UP LIKE THAT[8] AT SANTIAGO AIRPORT AND WE'LL BE IN JAIL[9] - OR WORSE - BEFORE YOU CAN BLINK[10]!
SORRY, I WASN'T THINKING[11].
HOW'S[12] LUCKY?
...
OH, THE DOG!
HE'S FINE. HE'S BEING LOOKED AFTER BY MRS BEACH[13], OUR NEIGHBOUR[14].

TOO SLOW.[1] IF YOU HAVE TO STOP AND THINK[2], THE ENEMY WILL KNOW YOU'RE LYING[3]. YOU HAVE TO TALK ABOUT YOUR DOG AND NEIGHBOURS AS IF YOU'VE KNOWN THEM ALL YOUR LIFE[4]!
I'M SORRY. I'M STILL JETLAGGED[5], THAT'S ALL.
SO HOW LONG HAVE YOU BEEN[6] WITH THE CIA?
THAT'S CLASSIFIED[7] INFORMATION.
WHO IS THE SALESMAN?
CLASSIFIED.
ALL RIGHT. IT'S PRETTY CLEAR[8] YOU DON'T WANT TO WORK WITH ME, AND THAT'S FINE[9], BECAUSE I DON'T WANT TO WORK WITH YOU.
FOR WHAT IT'S WORTH[10], NOBODY WOULD EVER[11] BELIEVE YOU'RE MY PARENTS, BECAUSE PARENTS WOULD NEVER BEHAVE[12] LIKE YOU TWO!
ALEX...
FORGET IT! I'M GOING BACK TO LONDON. YOU CAN TELL BYRNE I DIDN'T LIKE[13] THE JELLY, SO I WENT HOME[14] FOR[15] SOME JAM!
PLEASE, ALEX, SIT DOWN. YOU'RE RIGHT, WE WERE OUT OF LINE[16].
IT'S JUST GOING TO TAKE SOME TIME[17]. WE DON'T KNOW YOU.
RIGHT. IF YOU GET KILLED, HOW'S THAT GONNA MAKE US FEEL[18]?

1. Trop lent.
2. prendre le temps de réfléchir
3. que tu mens
4. comme si tu les connaissais depuis toujours
5. Je suis encore sous le coup du décalage horaire
6. depuis quand êtes-vous
7. classée secrète
8. C'est très clair
9. c'est parfait
10. De toute façon
11. jamais
12. ne se comporteraient jamais
13. que je n'ai pas aimé
14. alors je suis rentré chez moi
15. pour avoir
16. on a dépassé les bornes
17. un certain temps
18. comment on va le prendre

I WAS TOLD THERE WASN'T ANY DANGER. ANYWAY[1], I CAN LOOK AFTER MYSELF.
I DON'T BELIEVE THAT.[2]
WHATEVER.[3]
THE SALESMAN IS A CROOK[4], BASED HERE IN MIAMI. MEXICAN GUY[5], A NASTY PIECE OF WORK[6].
AND HE DOES JUST WHAT HIS NAME SAYS[7]. HE SELLS ANYTHING AND EVERYTHING[8].
DRUGS, WEAPONS[9], FALSE IDENTITIES[10], INFORMATION ... IF YOU NEED SOMETHING ILLEGAL, THE SALESMAN CAN SUPPLY IT[11].
AT A PRICE[12], OF COURSE.
I THOUGHT YOU WERE INVESTIGATING[13] SAROV.
WE ARE.[14] THE SALESMAN MAY HAVE SOLD[15] SOMETHING TO SAROV. THAT'S THE CONNECTION.
WHAT DID SAROV BUY?
WE DON'T KNOW FOR SURE[16].
ALL WE KNOW IS THAT TWO OF THE SALESMAN'S AGENTS FLEW INTO[17] SKELETON KEY RECENTLY AND NEVER RETURNED[18].
I'VE BEEN WORKING UNDERCOVER[19] WITH HIM FOR A WHILE[20], BUYING DRUGS. TODAY JUST HAPPENS TO BE[21] HIS BIRTHDAY, AND HE INVITED ME ON HIS BOAT.
SO YOU'RE GOING TO TRY AND FIND OUT[22] WHAT HE SOLD SAROV.
WHICH BOAT IS HIS[23]?

1. De toute façon
2. Ça m'étonnerait.
3. Enfin, bref.
4. escroc
5. Un Mexicain
6. un sale type
7. comme son nom l'indique
8. tout et n'importe quoi
9. des armes
10. des faux papiers
11. te le fournit
12. Moyennant un certain prix
13. que vous enquêtiez sur
14. C'est ce que nous faisons.
15. a peut-être vendu
16. de façon certaine
17. sont partis en avion à
18. ils ne sont jamais revenus
19. en m'infiltrant
20. depuis un moment
21. Il se trouve qu'aujourd'hui, c'est
22. essayer de découvrir
23. le sien

THAT ONE.[1]
WOW.
TIME FOR ME TO GO.[2]
I'LL STAY[3] WITH THE KID.
IT'S ONLY A TWENTY-MINUTE MEETING[4]. JUST EAT YOUR BREAKFAST AND WAIT HERE.

1. Celui-là.

2. Il faut que j'y aille.

3. Je reste

4. un rendez-vous de vingt minutes

WHAT DO WE DO[1] NOW?
WE WAIT.
SOMETHING'S WRONG.[2]
WHAT?
WHAT D'YOU MEAN?
THE BOAT'S LEAVING[3]!
BUT IT'S ONLY A TWENTY-MINUTE MEETING - TOM WASN'T MEANT TO[4] GO ANYWHERE[5]!
MAYBE HE CHANGED HIS MIND[6]. MAYBE THE SALESMAN INVITED HIM ON A CRUISE[7].
NOT WITHOUT ME. NOT WITHOUT COVER.[8] IT'S AGAINST COMPANY PROCEDURE[9]. NO...
HIS COVER'S BEEN BLOWN.[10]

1. Qu'est-ce qu'on fait

2. Il y a quelque chose qui va pas.

3. s'en va

4. Il n'était pas prévu que Tom

5. où que ce soit

6. qu'il a changé d'avis

7. croisière

8. Jamais sans se couvrir.

9. à l'encontre des principes de la maison

10. Sa couverture a sauté.

SO WHAT ARE YOU GOING TO DO?
I DON'T KNOW! IF THEY FIND OUT[1] WHO HE IS, THEY'LL KILL HIM!
THEN I'LL[2] DO SOMETHING.
NO, ALEX! WAIT!
HEY!
THAT BOARD[3] COST FIVE HUNDRED[4] DOLLARS!
SOMEBODY STOP[5]–
–WOAH!

1. découvrent

2. moi, je vais

3. skate

4. coûte cinq cents

5. Que quelqu'un l'arrête

OOF!
HOPE[1] NOBODY HEARD THAT...
LOOK AT[2] ALL THAT PETROL[3]! THE SALESMAN MUST BE PLANNING[4] ON BEING AWAY FOR SOME TIME...
WHICH ISN'T GOOD NEWS[5] FOR TURNER!

1. J'espère que

2. Regarde un peu

3. essence

4. doit avoir l'intention

5. une bonne nouvelle

YOU ARE A FOOLISH MAN[1]. YOUR NAME IS TOM TURNER. YOU WORK FOR THE CIA.
AND I AM GOING TO KILL YOU.
YOU'RE WRONG[2]...
I DON'T KNOW ... WHAT YOU'RE TALKING ABOUT.
I AM A VERY SUCCESSFUL MAN[3], MR TURNER. WHATEVER PEOPLE WANT, I SUPPLY. LIKE THIS RARE WINE[4], FOR EXAMPLE.
BUT I AM ALSO A CAREFUL MAN[5]. I MADE CERTAIN ... ENQUIRIES ABOUT YOU[6]. THE CIA WAS MENTIONED[7]. AND SO YOU ARE HERE.
WHAT DO YOU... WANT TO KNOW?
I WANT TO KNOW WHEN WE ARE ONE HOUR OUT OF[8] MIAMI...
...BECAUSE THAT IS WHEN I WILL SHOOT YOU[9] AND DUMP YOU OVER THE SIDE[10].

1. un idiot

2. Vous faites erreur

3. J'ai très bien réussi

4. vin

5. également très prudent

6. recherches vous concernant

7. évoquée

8. à une heure de

9. vous abattre

10. vous jeter par-dessus bord

TWO AGAINST[1] ONE, PLUS ALL THESE OTHER GUARDS, AND THEY ALL HAVE *GUNS*[2]. I NEED A *DIVERSION*...
...AND I KNOW JUST THE THING[3].
MMMMF!!!
TOO ... HEAVY[4]!
PETRO
NOTHING ELSE FOR IT...[5]
Rrrrrip

1. contre

2. ils sont tous armés

3. je sais exactement quoi

4. lourd

5. Y a pas d'autre solution...

...I'LL HAVE TO MAKE A FUSE INSTEAD[1].
HOPE THIS DOESN'T BLOW[2] THE WHOLE BOAT[3] SKYHIGH[4]...
ANOTHER GLASS[5], I THINK. YES.
BUT THEN I MUST LEAVE YOU[6]. I HAVE WORK TO—

1. plutôt fabriquer un détonateur

2. ne fera pas exploser

3. le bateau tout entier

4. jusqu'au ciel

5. verre

6. ensuite je devrai vous quitter

BOOM!
SEE[1] WHAT IS HAPPENING! QUICKLY![2]
¡SE PRENDIÓ LA GASOLINA![3]
¡TRAIGAN UN EXTINTOR![4] ¡ÓRALE![5]

1. Allez voir
2. Dépêchez-vous !
3. L'essence a pris feu !
4. Apportez un extincteur !
5. Allez !

Dit
Dit
SLAM!
WHAT...?
HAHA! A BOY!
WHAT ARE YOU GOING TO DO? CALL[1] 911?
SORRY, YOU'VE GOT THE WRONG NUMBER[2]...

1. Appeler le

2. c'est pas le bon numéro

...BUT THIS CALL'S FOR YOU[1]!
Dit
Thwip!
UNH!
IT'S ONLY A KNOCKOUT DART[2]. HE'LL BE FINE.[3]
I HEARD AN EXPLOSION! WAS THAT YOU?
YEAH. I SET THE BOAT ALIGHT.[4]
YOU SET FIRE TO THE BOAT? BUT WE'RE ON THE BOAT!
LOOK OUT![5]
Blam! Blam!
BOOM!

1. cet appel vous est destiné

2. une flèche neutralisante

3. Il s'en remettra.

4. J'ai mis le feu au bateau.

5. Attention !

THAT MUST HAVE BEEN THE SECOND PETROL CAN[1]!
KOF!
HOW MANY WERE THERE?
ONLY TWO[2] ... I THINK!
ALL RIGHT, COME ON! WE'RE GOING TO HAVE TO SWIM[3]!
¡AHÍ ESTÁN![4] ¡DETÉNGANLOS![5]
Brakka Brakka
COME ON, MOVE[6]!
¡DISPÁRENLES, IDIOTAS! ¡ÓRALE![7]
Splash!

1. bidon

2. Deux seulement

3. nager

4. Les voilà !

5. Arrêtez-les !

6. bouge

7. Tirez-leur dessus, bande d'idiots, allez !

Thum
Thum
Thum
HHHHHT!
YOU'RE CRAZY! YOU COULD HAVE GOTTEN US BOTH KILLED[1]!
I JUST[2] SAVED YOUR LIFE!
YOU THINK SO...?[3]
...THINK AGAIN![4]
Brakka
Brakka
!
WE'RE SITTING DUCKS[5]!
WE DON'T STAND A[6]—

1. nous faire tuer tous les deux

2. Je viens de

3. Tu crois ça ?

4. Réfléchis donc !

5. des cibles parfaites

6. On n'a aucune

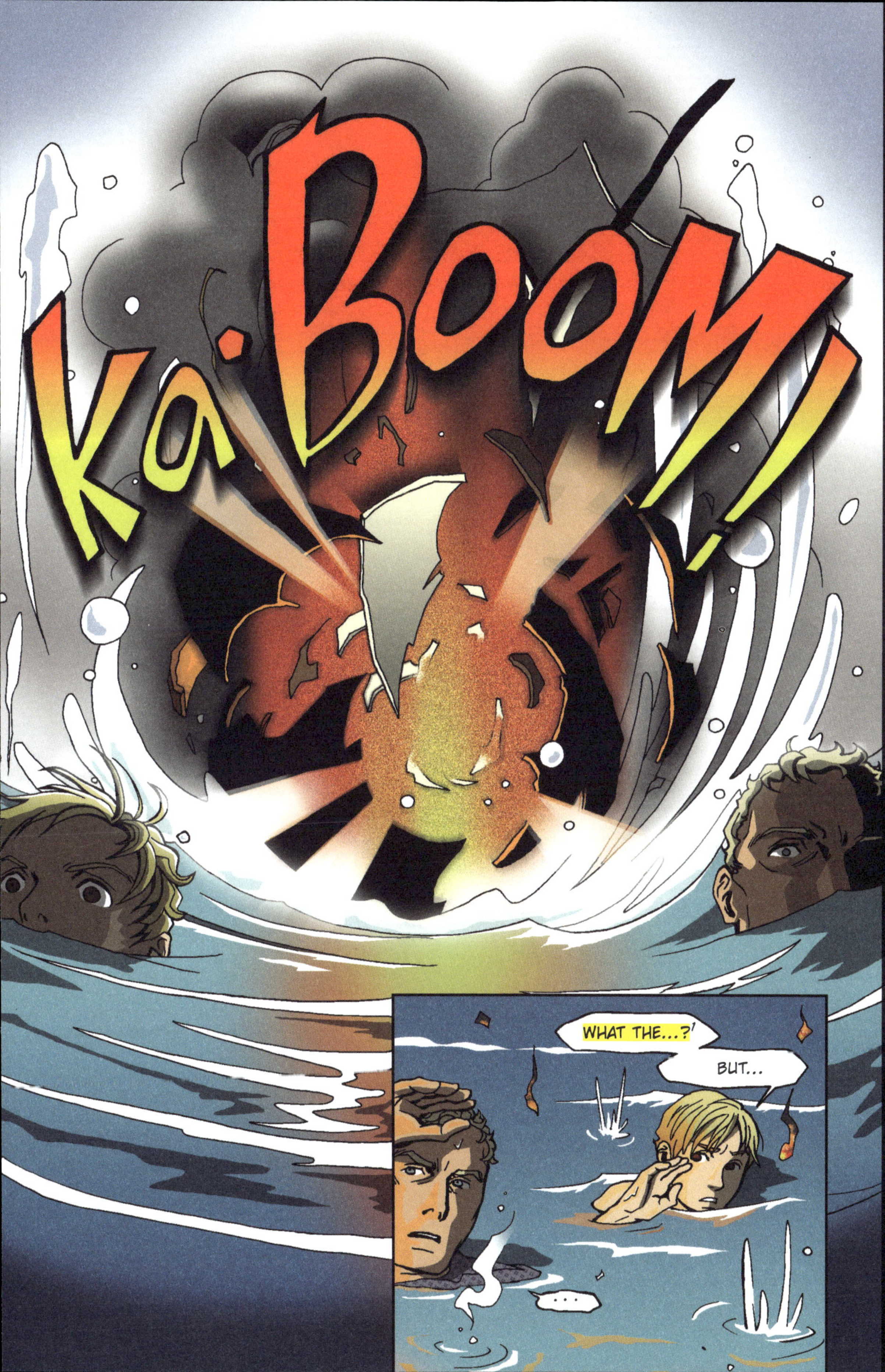
KA-BOOM!!
WHAT THE...?[1]
BUT...
...

1. Bon sang qu'est ce... ?

TOM!
ARE YOU ALL RIGHT?
WHAT HAPPENED? I SAW THE BOAT BLOW[1], AND I THOUGHT YOU WERE...
IT WAS THE KID!
HE BLEW UP[2] THE BOAT...
...AND KILLED THEM ALL IN THE PROCESS[4]!
NO!
I DIDN'T![3]
NO! THERE WASN'T ENOUGH PETROL TO DO THAT ... THEY WERE STARTING TO GET THE FIRE UNDER CONTROL[5]!
FOR GOD'S SAKE, KID! YOU THINK A LIGHT FUSE BLEW[6] AND TOOK THE BOAT WITH IT[7]?
YOU DID IT, ALEX. YOU SET THE GAS ALIGHT[8] AND THAT'S WHAT HAPPENED.
YOU KILLED THEM ALL.

1. exploser

2. Il a fait exploser

3. Ce n'est pas moi !

4. par la même occasion

5. à maîtriser le feu

6. qu'un fusible a sauté

7. emporté le bateau avec lui

8. tu as mis le feu à l'essence

SANTIAGO AIRPORT, CAYO ESQUELETO
PLEASE FASTEN YOUR SEAT-BELTS[1]. WE WILL SHORTLY BE COMING IN TO LAND.
PUT THE NINTENDO AWAY[2], ALEX. WE'RE[3] ALMOST AT THE FRONT OF THE LINE[4].
WHY DID YOU GIVE IT TO ME IF YOU DIDN'T WANT ME TO PLAY WITH IT? WE'VE BEEN WAITING HERE HOURS...[5]
DO AS YOUR MOTHER SAYS[6].
COME ON, THEY'RE CALLING US.
THE PURPOSE[7] OF YOUR VISIT, MR GARDINER?
VACATION.
SO MUCH FOR SECURITY.[8] THE GUARD'S HALF ASLEEP[9], AND THEY'VE ONLY GOT ONE CCTV[10] CAMERA!
ENJOY YOUR VISIT[11] TO CAYO ESQUELETO.
DON'T HOLD UP[12] THE LINE, ALEX.
THANK YOU.

1. attachez vos ceintures

2. Range la Nintendo

3. On arrive

4. de la file d'attente

5. Ça fait des heures qu'on attend...

6. ce que ta mère te dit

7. Le motif

8. Tu parles d'un système de sécurité.

9. à moitié endormi

10. de télé-surveillance

11. Bon séjour

12. Ne bloque pas

THIS IS[1] THE FAMILY?
YES. WHEN WE SEARCHED THEIR LUGGAGE WE FOUND A BOOKSTORE RECEIPT[2] - FROM LANGLEY[3], VIRGINIA[4].
WHERE THE CIA IS BASED.
EXACTLY. THEIR IMMIGRATION FORMS[5] ARE ON THE WAY TO OUR LABORATORY, TO ANALYSE THEIR FINGERPRINTS[6].
SHALL I[7] ARREST THEM NOW, JUST IN CASE?
NO ... NO, WE MUST BE SURE. WE CANNOT AFFORD[8] TO SCARE AWAY[9] GENUINE[10] TOURISTS.
LET THEM GO FOR NOW[11].
VERY WELL. I WILL SEND THEIR PICTURES[12] AND FINGERPRINTS TO THEIR HOTEL, THE POLICE...
AND OUR SPECIAL FRIEND[13] IN CASA DE ORO.

1. C'est celle-là

2. ticket de caisse d'une librairie

3. [ville où est installé le siège de la CIA]

4. [État de Virginie, USA]

5. formulaires d'immigration

6. empreintes digitales

7. Dois-je

8. nous permettre

9. de faire fuir

10. de vrais

11. pour l'instant

12. leurs photos

13. notre cher ami

VALENCIA HOTEL
WOW. THIS IS IMPRESSIVE[1].
CAN I GO FOR A SWIM[2]?
SURE THING[3], HONEY[4]! BUT YOU BE CAREFUL!
"SURE THING, HONEY..."
TROY SAID WE HAVE TO STAY IN CHARACTER[5] IN CASE THE HOTEL'S BUGGED[6], BUT IT REALLY DOESN'T SUIT HER[7].
OH WELL. ENJOY IT[8] WHILE I CAN[9], I GUESS[10]!

1. impressionnant
2. aller nager
3. Mais bien sûr
4. mon chéri
5. jouer notre rôle en permanence
6. serait truffé de micros
7. ça ne lui correspond vraiment pas
8. J'en profite
9. tant que je peux
10. je suppose

ONE HOUR LATER
I WONDER[1] WHAT IT WOULD HAVE BEEN LIKE IF MY REAL MUM[2] AND DAD[3] HAD LIVED[4].
AN ORDINARY LIFE[5], WORRYING ABOUT SCHOOLWORK[6], EXAMS[7] AND GIRLS ... NOT SPIES AND EXPLODING BOATS.
THEN AGAIN, I WOULDN'T BE SUNNING[8] IT IN A FIVE-STAR[9] HOTEL...
MOM? DAD?
NOT HERE[10] ... TIME FOR NINTENDO, THEN.
BUT I WONDER...
TURNER WAITED TILL WE WERE BOARDING[11] THE PLANE BEFORE HE GAVE ME THE DS. AND THEY DIDN'T WANT ME USING IT IN THE AIRPORT...
IS IT REALLY[12] A GADGET, LIKE THE ONE MI6 GAVE ME LAST YEAR[13]?

1. Je me demande

2. maman

3. papa

4. avaient vécu

5. Une vie normale

6. le travail scolaire

7. les examens

8. je ne serais pas en train de me dorer la pilule

9. cinq étoiles

10. Ils sont pas là

11. que nous montions à bord de

12. Et si c'était

13. l'année dernière

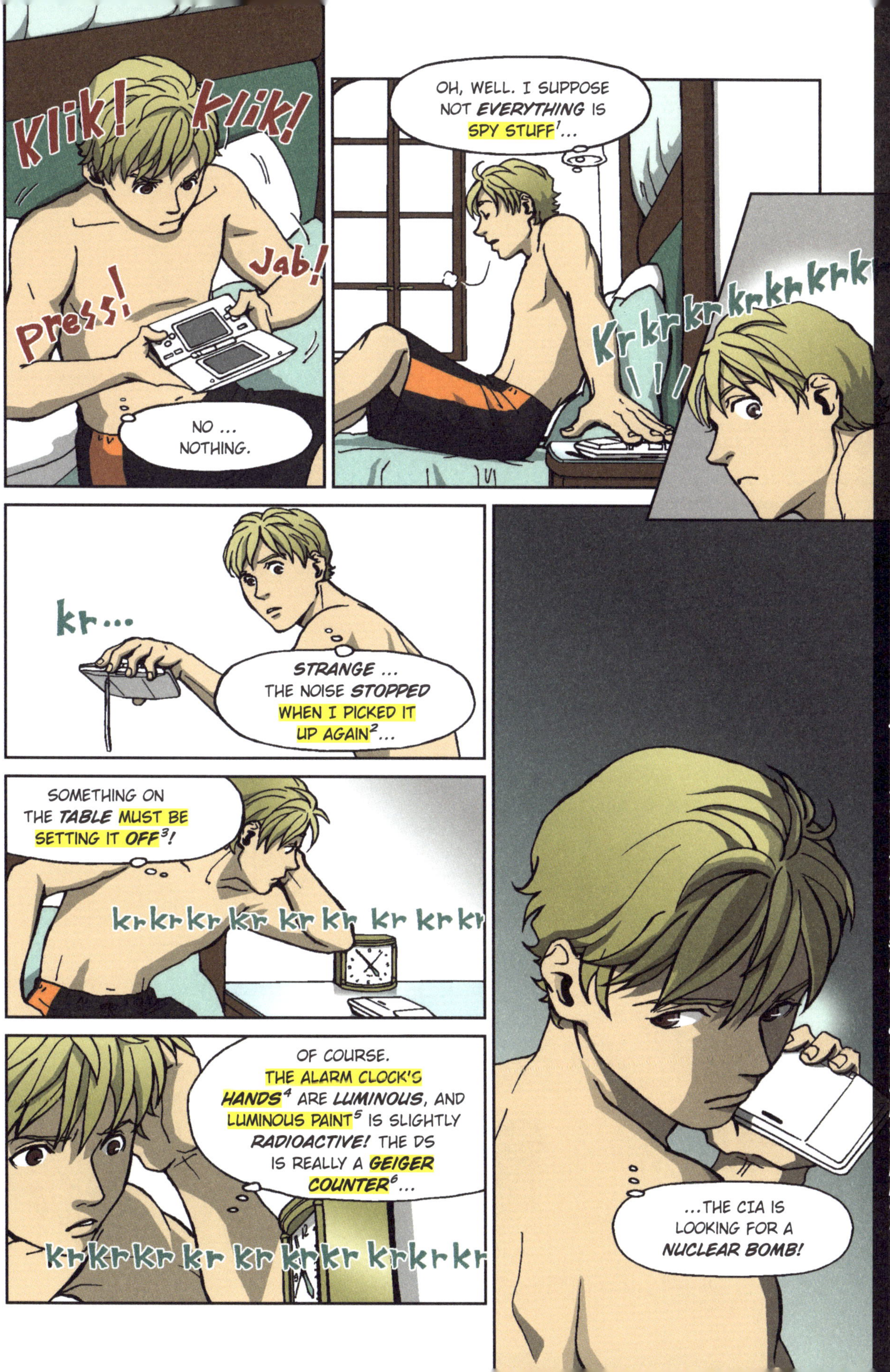
Klik! Klik!
Jab!
Press!
NO ... NOTHING.
OH, WELL. I SUPPOSE NOT EVERYTHING IS SPY STUFF[1]...
Krkrkrkrkrkrk
kr...
STRANGE ... THE NOISE STOPPED WHEN I PICKED IT UP AGAIN[2]...
SOMETHING ON THE TABLE MUST BE SETTING IT OFF[3]!
krkrkrkr kr kr kr krkr
OF COURSE. THE ALARM CLOCK'S HANDS[4] ARE LUMINOUS, AND LUMINOUS PAINT[5] IS SLIGHTLY RADIOACTIVE! THE DS IS REALLY A GEIGER COUNTER[6]...
krkrkr kr kr krkr krkrkr
...THE CIA IS LOOKING FOR A NUCLEAR BOMB!

1. du matos d'espionnage

2. quand je l'ai repris

3. doit le déclencher

4. Les aiguilles du réveil

5. la peinture lumineuse

6. compteur Geiger [détecteur de particules ionisantes, inventé par les physiciens Geiger et Müller]

YAWN
WOW, I OVERSLEPT[1]...
NEXT MORNING
...AND MY "PARENTS" COULDN'T EVEN BE BOTHERED[2] TO WAKE ME UP.
GONE FOR A WALK[3]
THOUGHT YOU NEEDED A REST
WE'LL CATCH UP WITH YOU[4] LATER
MOM XXX
THE NINTENDO'S GONE[5]...
THEY MUST HAVE SNUCK IN[6] AND TAKEN IT DURING THE NIGHT.
"GONE FOR A WALK" ... YEAH, RIGHT. WITH A GEIGER COUNTER. WELL, I'M NOT WAITING HERE ALL DAY. I MAY AS WELL[7] SEE[8] SOME OF THIS FAMOUS TOURIST SPOT[9].

1. j'ai dormi trop longtemps

2. n'ont même pas pris la peine

3. On est partis se promener

4. On se retrouve

5. n'est plus là

6. entrer discrètement

7. Pourquoi ne pas

8. visiter

9. site touristique

SO THIS IS
PUERTO MADRE.
"PLAZA DE FRATERNIDAD" ...
"BROTHERHOOD SQUARE".
YOU WANT CIGARS? BEST HAVANA CIGARS AT CHEAP[1], CHEAP PRICE!
HEY, AMIGO[2]! I SELL YOU A T-SHIRT!
MUCHACHO![3] YOU BRING[4] YOUR PARENTS TO MY BAR, EH?
NO, THANK YOU, I DON'T—
HEY!
THERE'S[5] TURNER AND TROY. BUT WHO'S THAT WITH THEM?

1. bon marché

2. mon ami

3. Petit !

4. Amène donc

5. Voilà

SORRY, AMIGOS, NOT TODAY...
ALEX!
WHAT ARE YOU DOING HERE? WE TOLD YOU TO STAY AT THE HOTEL!
YEAH, WELL[1], I THOUGHT THIS WAS MEANT TO BE A FAMILY[2] HOLIDAY.
I SEARCHED THE HOTEL BEFORE I LEFT[3], BY THE WAY[4], BUT I COULDN'T FIND ANY[5] NUCLEAR BOMBS.
!
KEEP YOUR VOICE DOWN![6]
YOU LIED[7] TO ME. YOU'RE NOT JUST SPYING ON[8] GENERAL SAROV, ARE YOU?[9]
WHY DON'T YOU TELL ME WHAT THIS IS REALLY ABOUT[10]?
...

1. Ouais, eh bien
2. en famille
3. avant de partir
4. au fait
5. je n'ai trouvé aucune
6. Parle à voix basse !
7. avez menti
8. On ne fait pas qu'espionner
9. n'est-ce pas ?
10. de quoi il s'agit réellement

ALL RIGHT. WE'LL TELL YOU WHAT WE CAN.
THAT'S AGAINST ORDERS[1]!
WHAT CHOICE DO WE HAVE? HE OBVIOUSLY[2] KNOWS ABOUT THE NINTENDO.
YOU MEAN[3] THE GEIGER COUNTER.
WE DIDN'T TELL YOU BECAUSE WE DIDN'T WANT TO FRIGHTEN YOU[4].
OH, HOW KIND[5].
WE WERE ORDERED NOT TO![6]
BUT YOU'RE RIGHT. WE BELIEVE THERE'S A NUCLEAR DEVICE[7] HIDDEN[8] ON THIS ISLAND.
AND YOU THINK SAROV HAS IT[9]?
WE SHOULDN'T BE TELLING HIM THIS. IT'S AGAINST PROTOCOL.
SHUT UP[10], TOM.
SOMETHING'S HAPPENING[11] HERE. WHILE WE WERE INVESTIGATING[12] THE SALESMAN, WE DISCOVERED HE'D GOT HIS HANDS ON[13] A KILO OF WEAPONS-GRADE URANIUM, OUT OF EASTERN EUROPE[14].

1. contraire à nos instructions

2. de toute évidence

3. Tu veux dire

4. t'effrayer

5. comme c'est gentil

6. On nous a ordonné de ne pas le faire !

7. engin nucléaire

8. caché

9. que c'est Sarov qui l'a

10. Ferme-la

11. Il se passe quelque chose

12. Alors que nous enquêtions sur

13. qu'il avait mis la main sur

14. en provenance d'Europe de l'Est

1. à qui il l'a vendu

2. collaborateurs

3. qu'ils l'ont livré

4. Et tout d'un coup

5. une rencontre

6. dans le tableau

7. nous aussi

8. Qu'est-ce qu'il a l'intention de faire avec ça ?

9. à quel point

10. nous introduire dans

11. et regarder partout

AND THE PERSON HE SOLD IT TO[1]...
...WAS GENERAL SAROV.
REMEMBER THOSE ASSOCIATES[2] OF THE SALESMAN WHO FLEW IN HERE BUT NEVER RETURNED? WE THINK THEY DELIVERED IT[3].
SO SUDDENLY[4] WE'VE GOT A MEETING[5] BETWEEN A GENERAL FROM OLD RUSSIA AND THE PRESIDENT OF NEW RUSSIA...
...AND THE POSSIBILITY OF A NUCLEAR WEAPON IN THE PICTURE[6].
EVERYONE IN WASHINGTON IS TERRIFIED. TO BE HONEST, SO ARE WE[7].
WHY?
WHAT'S HE PLANNING TO DO WITH IT?[8]
IF WE KNEW THAT, WE WOULDN'T BE HERE!
...I'M SORRY.
BUT NOW YOU SEE HOW[9] DANGEROUS THIS MISSION IS. WE HAVE TO BREAK INTO[10] CASA DE ORO AND LOOK AROUND[11].
...

IS THAT WHAT YOU WERE TALKING TO THAT MAN ABOUT[1]?
HIS NAME'S GARCIA.
HE'S ONE OF OUR "ASSETS[2]" HERE, WORKING FOR US AS AN INFORMANT[3] AND LOCAL HELP[4]. HE ALSO HAS A BOAT.
"CASA DE ORO IS BUILT ON A CLIFFTOP[5] AT THE TIP[6] OF THE ISLAND. IT'S AN OLD SUGAR CANE PLANTATION[7]. THEY EVEN HAVE A FULLY WORKING MILL[8].
"THERE'S ONLY ONE ROAD[9] INTO THE ESTATE[10]. IT'S NARROW[11], WITH A DROP ON BOTH SIDES[12], AND HEAVILY GUARDED[13]. WE'D NEVER GET IN[14] THAT WAY[15]."
BUT BY BOAT...
SCUBA[16], ACTUALLY.
SEE[17], WE KNOW SOMETHING SAROV DOESN'T. THERE'S A FAULT LINE[18] IN THE ROCK, A NATURAL SHAFT[19] THAT GOES ALL THE WAY UP[20] THE CLIFF.
AND YOU'RE GOING TO CLIMB IT[21]?
GARCIA'S FAMILY HAS BEEN ON THE ISLAND[22] FOR CENTURIES[23]. ACCORDING TO THEM[24], THREE HUNDRED YEARS AGO SMUGGLERS[25] BUILT METAL RUNGS[26] INTO THE SHAFT.

1. de ça que vous discutiez avec cet homme
2. agent double
3. informateur
4. soutien local
5. en haut d'une falaise
6. l'extrémité
7. ancienne plantation de canne à sucre
8. un moulin totalement opérationnel
9. route
10. pour entrer dans le domaine
11. étroite
12. un précipice de chaque côté
13. sous haute surveillance
14. entrer
15. par là
16. plongée sous-marine
17. Tu vois
18. ligne de faille
19. puits
20. remonte tout en haut de
21. l'escalader
22. habite sur cette île
23. des siècles
24. Selon eux
25. des contrebandiers
26. ont posé des anneaux en métal

THAT LADDER[1] RUNS UP[2] FROM A CAVE[3] AT THE BOTTOM[4] OF THE CLIFF, AND COMES OUT[5] IN THE GARDEN. THAT'S OUR WAY IN.[6]
THEY CALL IT THE DEVIL'S CHIMNEY[7].
WHERE DOES SCUBA DIVING COME INTO IT[8]?
THE WATER LEVEL'S HIGHER NOW, SO THE CAVE IS UNDERWATER[9]. MOST[10] PEOPLE HAVE FORGOTTEN IT EVER EXISTED[11].
SO YOU SWIM INTO[12] THE CAVE, CLIMB THE DEVIL'S CHIMNEY, AND SEARCH THE ESTATE[13].
WHAT HAPPENS IF YOU DO FIND A BOMB[14]?
NOT OUR PROBLEM. BY THEN, OUR WORK WILL BE DONE[15].
I SEE. IT'S A GOOD PLAN...
THANK YOU.
...SO[16] I'M COMING WITH YOU.
!

1. échelle
2. remonte
3. grotte
4. située au pied
5. ressort
6. C'est par là que nous entrons.
7. la cheminée du diable
8. entre en jeu
9. submergée
10. La plupart des
11. son existence
12. vous entrez à la nage dans
13. toute la propriété
14. vous découvrez réellement une bombe
15. accompli
16. Donc

NO WAY![1]
I TOLD YOU ALL THIS SO YOU'D UNDERSTAND HOW DANGEROUS IT IS! THIS ISN'T A VIDEOGAME[2], ZAPPING[3] BAD GUYS ON A SCREEN[4]! THIS IS THE REAL THING![5]
AND THIS IS A FAMILY HOLIDAY.
YOU KEEP DUMPING ME ON MY OWN[6] IN THE HOTEL, SOMEBODY'S GOING TO NOTICE[7] ... AND WONDER WHERE YOU BOTH ARE[8].
I'M NOT ASKING TO DIVE, OR CLIMB THE CHIMNEY. BUT IF WE'RE ALL ON THE BOAT, IT'LL LOOK MORE LIKE[9] A FAMILY CRUISE.
YOU KNOW, HE'S GOT A POINT[10].
ALL RIGHT. BUT YOU STAY OUT OF OUR WAY[11], AND IN THE BOAT WITH GARCIA. THAT'S FINAL.[12]
FINE. SO WHEN DO WE GO?
RIGHT NOW.[13] WE'RE DOING IT TONIGHT[14].

1. Hors de question !

2. jeu vidéo

3. où on élimine

4. sur un écran

5. Ça, c'est la réalité !

6. Si vous continuez à me laisser en plan

7. va le remarquer

8. où vous pouvez bien être, vous deux

9. ça ressemblera plus à

10. il a raison

11. à l'écart

12. Ce n'est pas négociable.

13. Tout de suite.

14. cette nuit

LATER
WE'LL DIVE HERE[1] AND SWIM UNDERWATER TO THE COAST[2].
WE'RE BEING WATCHED.[3]
DOESN'T MATTER.
DIVE BOATS[4] COME OUT HERE ALL THE TIME, EVEN THOUGH THEY[5] AREN'T SUPPOSED TO[6].
THERE'S AN OLD WRECK[7] AROUND HERE[8] THAT PEOPLE LIKE TO SWIM AROUND. THE GUARDS ARE USED TO IT[9].
WE'LL BE FINE, PROVIDED WE DON'T DRAW[10] ATTENTION TO OURSELVES[11].

1. On va plonger ici
2. jusqu'à la côte
3. On nous surveille.
4. Des bateaux de plongée
5. même s'ils
6. censés le faire
7. épave
8. par ici
9. y sont habitués
10. pourvu qu'on attire pas
11. sur nous

WE'LL START WITH AN EXPLORATORY DIVE[1]. TWENTY MINUTES, NO LONGER[2].
ALL WE NEED TO DO IS FIND THE CAVE AND CHECK[3] THERE ARE NO SECURITY DEVICES[4].
THEN WE'LL COME BACK FOR[5] THE REST OF OUR EQUIPMENT, CHANGE AIR TANKS[6] AND GO BACK WHEN IT'S DARK[7].
YOU'RE NOT TAKING THE NINTENDO?
WON'T NEED IT UNTIL WE GET BACK.
YOU KNOW, I'M A QUALIFIED DIVER[8]...
THE HELL WITH THAT![9]
YOU TALKED YOUR WAY ONTO[10] THE BOAT, BUT YOU ARE NOT DIVING. JUST SIT TIGHT[11] AND WAIT HERE.

1. une plongée d'exploration

2. pas plus

3. vérifier

4. d'équipements de sécurité

5. pour récupérer

6. les bouteilles d'oxygène

7. quand il fera nuit

8. un bon plongeur

9. Je m'en fiche !

10. Tu nous as persuadés de te laisser venir sur

11. Contente-toi de te tenir tranquille

YOU AMERICAN?
ENGLISH.
SO WHY YOU HERE?
I'VE BEEN ASKING MYSELF[1] THE SAME[2] QUESTION.
YOU KNOW WHY THEY DON'T LIKE YOU[3]?

1. Je me pose

2. même

3. ils ne t'aiment pas

THEY ARE GROWN-UPS[1]. THEY THINK THEY GOOD AT WHAT THEY DO[2]. BUT THEN ALONG COMES[3] A CHILD, AND HE IS BETTER[4].
WORSE[5], HE IS ENGLISH!
I DIDN'T ASK TO BE HERE.
BUT STILL[6] YOU CAME.
THEY'VE BEEN GONE TOO LONG[7]. THEY'LL RUN OUT[8] OF AIR SOON[9].
MAYBE[10] THEY ENTER DEVIL'S CHIMNEY. CLIMB UP!
NO. THAT WASN'T THE PLAN, REMEMBER?
DIDN'T THEY HAVE A BACKUP PLAN[11]? WHAT DID THEY TELL YOU TO DO?
THEY TELL ME TO WAIT. SO I WAIT AN HOUR, TWO HOURS, I WAIT ALL NIGHT.
WELL, I'M NOT WAITING[12].
HAVE YOU GOT ANY MORE SCUBA GEAR[13]?

1. des adultes

2. qu'ils font bien leur travail

3. voilà qu'arrive

4. plus doué

5. Pire

6. quand même

7. depuis trop longtemps

8. Ils vont manquer

9. bientôt

10. Peut-être

11. un plan de secours

12. moi, j'attends pas

13. d'autres équipements de plongée

FIVE MINUTES LATER
YOU SHOULD NOT DIVE ALONE[1].
AS IF YOU'RE GOING TO[2] COME WITH ME.
OF COURSE NOT. BUT TAKE THIS.
IN CASE, YOU KNOW?
THANKS. SEE YOU SOON!
Splash!
Thud
OUCH!
I'M OUT OF PRACTICE[3] ... BUT NEVER MIND[4]. I HAVE TO FIND THAT CAVE. AND QUICKLY, BEFORE IT'S TOO DARK[5] TO SEE.

1. plonger seul

2. Comme si vous alliez

3. Je manque d'entraînement

4. tant pis

5. trop sombre

THERE IT IS. MAYBE THEY'RE WAITING INSIDE[1] AFTER ALL...
BRRR, CREEPY[2].
NO SIGN[3] OF TURNER AND TROY, BUT I'D BETTER[4] GO IN AND FIND THE LADDER, JUST IN CASE...
WHAT WAS THAT?[5]
SOMETHING BIG...
OH, NO!
A GREAT WHITE SHARK[6]!

1. à l'intérieur

2. flippant

3. Aucune trace

4. je ferais mieux de

5. C'était quoi, ça ?

6. requin blanc

1. il fait des cercles autour de moi

2. Ma bouteille de plongée

3. je ne porte pas

4. des vêtements de couleur vive

5. Je me suis fait une coupure au bras

6. Il sent

7. cambre

8. dos

BUT WHY'S IT CIRCLING ME[1]?
MY CYLINDER[2]'S BLACK, I'M NOT WEARING[3] BRIGHT CLOTHES[4]...
OH, NO.
I CUT MY ARM[5] WHEN I DIVED IN! IT CAN SMELL[6] MY BLOOD!
IT'S ARCHING[7] ITS BACK[8] ... IT'S GOING TO...
...ATTACK!

IT'S TURNING TO ATTACK AGAIN. ONLY GOT ONE[1] CHANCE...
Stab!
Nnngh!
BARELY A SCRATCH.[2] AND NOW IT'S COMING BACK!
GOT TO[3] GET IN THE CAVE, GET OUT[4] OF THE WATER...
...TOO LATE!

1. Je n'ai qu'une seule

2. À peine une égratignure.

3. Je dois

4. sortir

bzzzzzzzzz..
Krump!
WHAT THE...?

bzzzzzzz!...
THE STALACTITES AND STALAGMITES ARE FAKE[1]... THE WHOLE CAVE[2] IS A TRAP[3]!
AND IT EVEN HAS ITS OWN DISPOSAL SYSTEM[4]. GROSS.[5]
THERE MUST BE AN INFRA-RED BEAM[6] TO ACTIVATE IT. THE SHARK BROKE THE BEAM[7]...
AND I'LL BET TURNER AND TROY DID, TOO[8].
TIME TO[9] GET OUT OF HERE. THIS WHOLE MISSION[10] IS A DISASTER!
HAAAAAH!

1. sont fausses

2. La grotte tout entière

3. piège

4. système d'élimination

5. Dégueu.

6. un faisceau infrarouge

7. a traversé le faisceau

8. ont fait pareil

9. Il est temps de

10. Toute cette mission

1. c'est bon, ne m'aidez pas

2. sont morts

3. fiasco

4. que vous me rameniez

5. Est-ce que vous écoutez

MMMF!
NO, DON'T BOTHER HELPING[1], I'M FINE...
GARCIA, WE HAVE TO GO. TURNER AND TROY ARE DEAD[2], AND THE MISSION'S A BUST[3].
DO YOU UNDERSTAND? YOU HAVE TO TAKE ME BACK[4] TO THE HOTEL!
GARCIA! ARE YOU LISTENING[5]—
OH, NO...
NO, NO, NO...
YESH.
Whack!

OHN OCHNISHSYA.
!
HEY! LET ME OUT[1] OF HERE! WHAT'S GOING ON?
YOOR NAAAME[2]?
ALEX GARDINER!
YOO LIE.[3] YOOR REAL[4] NAAAME IZH[5] ALEX RRRIDER.
WHY ASK[6] IF YOU THINK YOU ALREADY KNOW?
MY NAAAME IZH KHONRAD.

1. Laissez-moi sortir

2. nom

3. Tu mens.

4. vrai

5. est

6. Pourquoi me le demander

WE HAVVVE MET BEEEFORE.[1]
!
WHYYY ARE YOO HEEERE?
I'M ON VACATION[2] WITH MY MOM AND DAD. WHERE ARE THEY? WHY HAVE YOU BROUGHT ME HERE? I WANT TO GO HOME!
YOOR ACCENNT[3] IZH VERY GOOOD, BUT YOO ARE ENGLISHHH. YOOR "PAARENTS" WERE CIA AGENNTS. THEY ARE DEADD.
I MUSSHT[4] KNOW WHYYY YOOO ARE HEERE.
I ALREADY TOLD YOU, I'M ON VACATION! I DON'T KNOW WHAT YOU'RE TALKING ABOUT[5]!
SIGH[6]
VERY WELLL.
klik

1. On s'est déjà rencontrés.

2. en vacances

3. Ton accent

4. Je dois

5. de quoi vous parlez

6. soupir

THISH PLACE WAS ONNNCE A SSHUGAR MILL[1]. SSHUGAR CAAANE WAS DELLIVERED[2] HEERE BY FARRRMERS[3]. IT WAS SHHREDDED[4] ANND PLACED ON A BELLLT[5] TO BE CRUSHHED[6].
OH, NO...
Gr...
THENN IT WAS FILLTERED[7], ANND THEE REMAINNNING SYRUP[8] WAS PLACED IN CAULLLDRONS[9] ANND HEATED[10] TO FORM CRYSTALLLS[11].
Grrrrnd
YOOO ARE AT THEE START OF THEE PROCESHH[12]. IMAGINNE THE PAAAIN THAT LIES AHEADD OF YOO[13].
FIRRRST YOOR TOES[14], THEN YOOR FEET[15] ... ONE CENTIMMMETRE AT A TIME[16].
HOWW MUCH OF YOOO[17] WILL BE PROCESSHED[18] BEFORE YOO ARRE ALLOWED THEE COMFFFORT OF DEATH[19]?
Grrrrrrrrrnd...
SWITCH IT OFF![20] STOP IT!
TELL MEE WHAT I WANNNT TO KNOWW, AND I WILL PRESH[21] THEE RED BUTTONN TOO SHTOP THEE MACHINNNE.
YOU'RE WRONG![22] YOU CAN'T DO THIS!

1. une sucrerie

2. était livrée

3. par les paysans

4. broyée

5. sur un tapis roulant

6. pressée

7. filtrée

8. le sirop extrait

9. des chaudrons

10. chauffé

11. des cristaux

12. au début du processus

13. la souffrance qui t'attend

14. orteils

15. pieds

16. à la fois

17. Quelle proportion de ton corps

18. débitée

19. avant que la mort ne vienne te délivrer

20. Coupez-le !

21. j'appuierai sur

22. Vous vous trompez !

1. Ne perds pas
2. Il t'en reste si peu...
3. le laisser faire ça
4. Qu'est-ce que ces agents savaient au juste ?
5. tout le reste
6. Continue.
7. sous couverture
8. avait acheté
9. le convoyeur

I AM DOING THISH. ANND I AM NEVVVER WRONNNG.
DOO NOT WASHTE[1] ANNNY MOORE TIME. YOOO HAVE SO LITTLE OF IT LEFFFT...[2]
STOP HIM! YOU CAN'T LET HIM DO THIS[3]! I'M JUST A BOY!
HOW MUCH DIDD THEE AGENTSH KNOWW?[4] WHYY WERRRE THEY HEERE?
PLEASE...
Grrrrrrrrnd..
ALL RIGHT!
YOU ALREADY KNOW EVERYTHING ELSE[5], SO WHAT DIFFERENCE DOES IT MAKE? THEY WERE LOOKING FOR A NUCLEAR BOMB!
GO ONN.[6]
TURNER WAS WORKING UNDERCOVER[7] AND FOUND OUT THAT SAROV BOUGHT[8] URANIUM FROM THE SALESMAN! THEY CAME HERE TO FIND IT!
NOW STOP THE CONVEYOR[9]!

NNOT YETT.[1]
DID THEYY KNOW THEE PURPOSHE[2] OF THEE BOMMMB?
NO! THEY DIDN'T TELL ME!
PLEASE, STOP...
...NO.
WHAT?!
YOOO'VE BEEN A BADD BOY[3] ... ANND BADD BOYSH MUST BEE PUNISHHHED[4].
BUT YOU SAID! YOU SAID YOU WOULD[5]!
I LIED.[6]
NO!
JUSHT[7] LIKE YOOO.
NOOOOOOOOO

1. Pas tout de suite.

2. l'objectif

3. vilain garçon

4. doivent être punis

5. que vous le feriez

6. J'ai menti.

7. Exactement

BLAM!
Krak!
Grrrrr....
...
HHH ... HHH—
MY DEAR[1] ALEX, I'M SO SORRY. ARE YOU ALL RIGHT?
HE IS UNCONSCIOUS ... BUT ALIVE[2]. BRING HIM[3] TO THE HOUSE!

1. Mon cher

2. vivant

3. Amenez-le

ALEX?
....
AH, YOU ARE WAKING UP[1].
YOU MUST FORGIVE[2] CONRAD. HE IS AN EXCELLENT ASSISTANT, AND USEFUL[3] IN MANY WAYS[4]. BUT HE CAN BE ... OVER-ENTHUSIASTIC.
CASA DE ORO
HE HAD NO ORDERS TO ELIMINATE YOU. ON THE CONTRARY, WHEN I FOUND OUT WHO YOU WERE, I VERY MUCH WANTED TO[5] MEET YOU.
HOW DID YOU FIND OUT?
CONTRARY TO APPEARANCES[6], WE HAVE A VERY SOPHISTICATED SECURITY SYSTEM HERE, AND IN HAVANA.
NOW, YOU HAVE HAD A TERRIBLE ORDEAL[7]—
TURNER AND TROY HAD A WORSE ONE[8].
YES...
OF COURSE I WAS AWARE[9] OF THE DEVIL'S CHIMNEY WHEN I BOUGHT THIS HOUSE. I CONSTRUCTED A SIMPLE DEFENCE MECHANISM.
THEY TELL ME IT ALSO KILLED A SHARK TODAY.

1. tu es réveillé

2. pardonner

3. utile

4. à maints égards

5. je voulais vraiment

6. En dépit des apparences

7. une terrible épreuve

8. ont vécu pire

9. j'étais au courant

IT DID. A GREAT WHITE[1].
YOU SAW IT? AND SURVIVED[2]?
YOU ARE AS REMARKABLE AS YOUR FILE SAYS[3].
SOME WOULD SAY YOU HAVE THE LUCK OF THE DEVIL[4] ... THOUGH I DO NOT BELIEVE IN THE DEVIL, OR GOD FOR THAT MATTER[5].
BUT I BELIEVE IN YOU, ALEX RIDER. YOU ARE QUITE[6] UNIQUE.
WHY AM I HERE? WHAT DO YOU WANT WITH ME?[7]
YOU ARE HERE BECAUSE I CANNOT LET YOU LEAVE[8]. CASA DE ORO IS YOUR PRISON, THOUGH I HOPE YOU WILL FIND IT COMFORTABLE. AS FOR[9] WHAT I WANT WITH YOU...
IT IS LATE.
WE WILL TALK MORE TOMORROW.
DO YOU REALLY HAVE A NUCLEAR BOMB? MADE FROM[10] THE URANIUM THE SALESMAN SOLD YOU?
YES. BUT HE IS NO LONGER A CONCERN[11]. I HAD CONRAD[12] BLOW UP HIS BOAT.
CONRAD? SO IT WASN'T ME! I KNEW IT!
WHAT ARE YOU GOING TO DO WITH THE BOMB?
ARE YOU AFRAID?[13]

1. grand blanc
2. tu as survécu
3. que ton dossier le dit
4. une satanée chance
5. ni à Dieu, d'ailleurs
6. vraiment
7. Que me voulez-vous ?
8. te laisser partir
9. Quant à
10. Fabriquée avec
11. problème
12. J'ai demandé à Conrad de
13. Tu as peur ?

I JUST WANT TO KNOW.
OF COURSE.
I WILL TELL YOU THIS: MY COUNTRY WAS ONCE[1] A WORLD POWER[2], ONE OF THE MOST POWERFUL NATIONS ON EARTH[3].
"WE PUT[4] THE FIRST MAN INTO SPACE[5]. WE MADE THE GREATEST ADVANCES[6] IN SCIENCE AND TECHNOLOGY.
"WE WERE FEARED[7] BY THE REST OF THE WORLD!
"BUT COMMUNISM HAS BEEN DRIVEN OUT[8]. AND IN ITS ABSENCE, RUSSIA HAS BECOME SECOND-RATE[9], WITH NO LAW[10] AND ORDER.
"PRISONS ARE EMPTY[11]. CRIMINALS CONTROL THE STREETS[12]. MILLIONS ARE ADDICTED TO DRUGS[13], AND MILLIONS MORE HAVE AIDS[14]. WOMEN AND CHILDREN WORK AS PROSTITUTES[15]."
AND WHY?
SO[16] THE PEOPLE CAN EAT[17] MCDONALD'S AND BUY LEVI JEANS AND TALK ON THEIR MOBILE TELEPHONES IN RED SQUARE[18]!
OK, I CAN SEE[19] YOU'RE ANGRY[20]...
BUT HOW IS A NUCLEAR BOMB GOING TO CHANGE ANY OF THAT[21]?

1. était autrefois
2. puissance mondiale
3. sur terre
4. Nous avons envoyé
5. dans l'espace
6. les plus grands progrès
7. Nous étions redoutés
8. a été chassé
9. un pays de seconde zone
10. sans loi
11. vides
12. les rues
13. sont dépendantes de la drogue
14. le sida
15. se prostituent
16. Pour que
17. puissent manger du
18. [la place Rouge, célèbre place au centre de Moscou, en Russie]
19. je vois
20. en colère
21. y changer quoi que ce soit

1. Je vais réparer le mal

2. trente dernières

3. Je rendrai à mon pays

4. prestige

5. sur la scène internationale

6. maléfique

7. Quoi que

8. aient pu te raconter

9. mon seul souhait

10. maladie

11. Il est très important pour moi

12. tu parviennes à

13. de mon point de vue

14. Nous prendrons le petit déjeuner

15. neuf heures du matin

16. je te ferai visiter

17. de t'enfuir

18. aucun moyen de descendre

19. fermée à clé

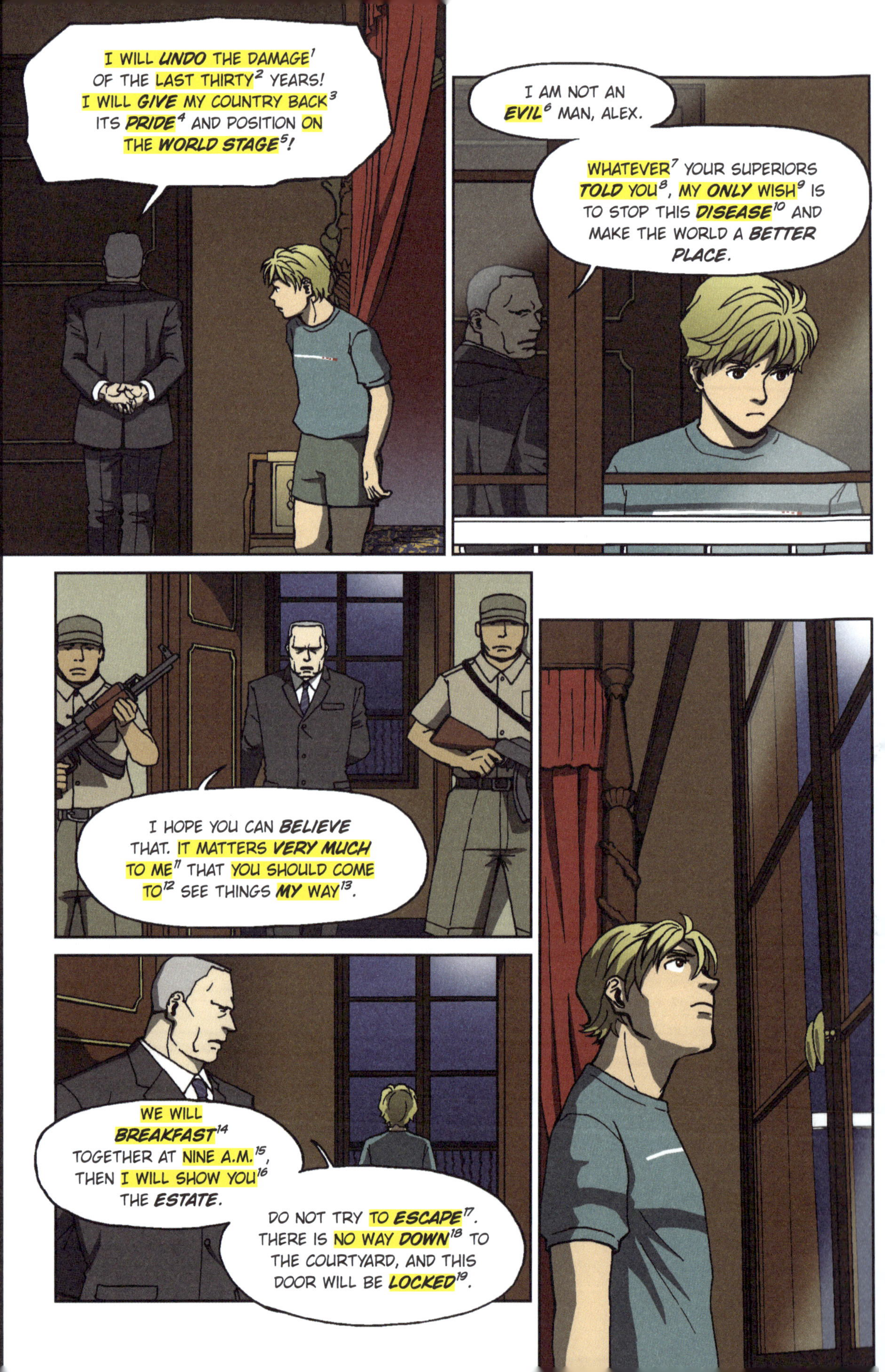

I WILL UNDO THE DAMAGE[1] OF THE LAST THIRTY[2] YEARS! I WILL GIVE MY COUNTRY BACK[3] ITS PRIDE[4] AND POSITION ON THE WORLD STAGE[5]!
I AM NOT AN EVIL[6] MAN, ALEX.
WHATEVER[7] YOUR SUPERIORS TOLD YOU[8], MY ONLY WISH[9] IS TO STOP THIS DISEASE[10] AND MAKE THE WORLD A BETTER PLACE.
I HOPE YOU CAN BELIEVE THAT. IT MATTERS VERY MUCH TO ME[11] THAT YOU SHOULD COME TO[12] SEE THINGS MY WAY[13].
WE WILL BREAKFAST[14] TOGETHER AT NINE A.M.[15], THEN I WILL SHOW YOU[16] THE ESTATE.
DO NOT TRY TO ESCAPE[17]. THERE IS NO WAY DOWN[18] TO THE COURTYARD, AND THIS DOOR WILL BE LOCKED[19].

SU PORTAFOLIOS[1], JOVEN[2].
MY LUGGAGE[3]...
SAROV MUST HAVE SENT SOMEONE TO THE *HOTEL* TO COLLECT IT[4]. I WONDER IF SMITHERS' *PHONE* IS STILL THERE?
NEXT MORNING
NO. BUT THE *OWEN FIGURE*[5] AND *CHEWING GUM* ARE[6]!
HMMM...
BETTER *NOT* WEAR[7] MY *LEVIS*.

1. Votre mallette

2. jeune homme

3. bagages

4. pour les récupérer

5. la figurine d'Owen

6. sont là

7. Je ferais mieux de ne pas mettre

IN HEEERE.
GOOD MORNING, ALEX.
FORGIVE MY CLOTHES[1]. I ALWAYS TAKE A TWENTY-FOUR MILE[2] RUN[3] BEFORE BREAKFAST. THREE TIMES AROUND[4] THE PLANTATION.
THAT WILL BE ALL[5], CONRAD. WE'LL MEET AGAIN AT MIDDAY[6].
CONRAD DOESN'T LIKE YOU.
THAT'S ALL RIGHT, I'M NOT CRAZY ABOUT[7] CONRAD.
WHAT'S THE MATTER WITH HIM[8], ANYWAY?
HE WAS INVOLVED[9] IN AN EXPLOSION ... WITH A BOMB THAT HE HAPPENED TO BE CARRYING[10] AT THE TIME.
HE IS A SCIENTIFIC MIRACLE. THERE ARE THIRTY METAL PINS[11] IN HIS BODY, A METAL PLATE[12] IN HIS SKULL[13], AND WIRES[14] IN HIS JAW[15] AND MOST OF HIS MAJOR JOINTS[16].
I BET HE'S A RIOT[17] AT AIRPORT SECURITY.
I WOULD ADVISE YOU[18] NOT TO MOCK HIM[19], ALEX. HE STILL VERY MUCH HOPES TO KILL YOU.
NOW, I HAVE REMOVED[20] YOUR MOBILE, AND ALL PHONES IN THE COMPOUND REQUIRE A CODE[21]. YOU CANNOT CONTACT THE OUTSIDE WORLD[22].

1. ma tenue

2. de trente-huit kilomètres

3. un jogging

4. Trois fois le tour de

5. Ce sera tout

6. midi

7. j'ai du mal avec

8. Qu'est-ce qui lui est arrivé

9. Il a été victime

10. qu'il transportait, justement

11. trente broches métalliques

12. plaque

13. crâne

14. des fils

15. mâchoire

16. principales articulations

17. Ça doit être tordant

18. Je te conseille

19. te moquer de lui

20. j'ai confisqué

21. exigent un code

22. le monde extérieur

MY PEOPLE MAY WORRY ABOUT ME[1].
FROM WHAT I KNOW[2] OF ALAN BLUNT AND HIS COLLEAGUES, THAT IS UNLIKELY[3]. BESIDES[4], BY THE TIME THEY BEGIN TO ASK QUESTIONS, IT WILL BE TOO LATE.
TOO LATE? FOR WHAT?
CASA DE ORO IS SURROUNDED[5] BY AN ELECTRIC FENCE[6]. THERE IS ONLY ONE ENTRANCE[7], AND IT IS ALWAYS GUARDED[8].
IF YOU ATTEMPT[9] TO ESCAPE, YOU WILL BE SHOT[10], AND THAT IS NOT AT ALL WHAT I HAVE PLANNED[11].
TODAY YOU WILL MOVE TO NEW QUARTERS[12]. I HAVE IMPORTANT GUESTS[13] ARRIVING, AND IT WOULD BE BETTER FOR YOU TO HAVE YOUR OWN SPACE[14].
YOU ARE STILL WELCOME TO USE[15] THE HOUSE, POOL[16], AND GROUNDS[17]. BUT IF YOU CAUSE ME ANY EMBARRASSMENT[18], I WILL HAVE YOU WHIPPED[19].
NOW, ENOUGH OF THIS UNPLEASANTNESS[20]. WE HAVE THE WHOLE MORNING[21] TOGETHER.
CAN YOU RIDE A HORSE?[22]

1. s'inquiéter pour moi
2. D'après ce que je sais
3. peu probable
4. En plus
5. entourée
6. clôture électrique
7. entrée
8. surveillée
9. Si tu tentes
10. on te tirera dessus
11. ce que j'ai prévu
12. tu emménageras dans de nouveaux quartiers
13. invités
14. ton propre espace
15. Tu peux tout de même profiter de
16. de la piscine
17. du domaine
18. le moindre ennui
19. je te ferai fouetter
20. ces choses déplaisantes
21. toute la matinée
22. Tu sais monter à cheval ?

LATER
THIS WAS ONCE A SUGAR FARM[1], WORKED BY SLAVES[2]. THERE WERE ALMOST A MILLION SLAVES IN CUBA AND CAYO ESQUELETO.
AT FOUR-THIRTY EVERY MORNING THEY WOULD RING A BELL UP THERE[3], FOR THE SLAVES TO START WORK. THEY ALL CAME FROM WEST AFRICA[4].
THEY WORKED HERE … AND THEY DIED[5] HERE.
THAT BUILDING IS THE BARRACÓN[6], THE HOUSE OF SLAVES. TWO HUNDRED OF THEM SLEPT IN THERE, PENNED IN[7] LIKE ANIMALS.
IF WE HAVE TIME, I WILL SHOW YOU THE PUNISHMENT BLOCK[8]. CAN YOU IMAGINE BEING FASTENED[9] BY YOUR ANKLES[10] FOR WEEKS, UNABLE TO[11] MOVE, STARVING AND THIRSTY[12]?
I DON'T WANT TO IMAGINE IT.
OF COURSE NOT. THE WESTERN WORLD[13] PREFERS TO FORGET THE CRIMES THAT MADE IT RICH[14].
YAAA!
HE KILLED TURNER AND TROY WITHOUT A THOUGHT[15] … BUT HE WANTS ME ALIVE[16].
WHY?

1. plantation de canne à sucre

2. où travaillaient des esclaves

3. une cloche, là-haut, sonnait

4. d'Afrique de l'Ouest

5. ils mouraient

6. baraquement

7. ils y étaient parqués

8. le quartier disciplinaire

9. être attaché

10. chevilles

11. sans pouvoir

12. mourant de faim et de soif

13. Le monde occidental

14. qui l'ont enrichi

15. sans réfléchir

16. que je reste en vie

I WISH[1] TO TELL YOU SOMETHING ABOUT MYSELF[2].
IN FACT, I WILL TELL YOU MORE[3] THAN I HAVE TOLD ANYONE ELSE[4].
I WAS BORN[5] DURING THE SECOND WORLD WAR[6], AS[7] THE GERMANS ATTACKED MY COUNTRY. PERHAPS THAT IS WHY I HAVE ALWAYS BEEN A PATRIOT.
I ALWAYS BELIEVED MY COUNTRY COMES FIRST[8]. I HAVE SPENT MUCH OF MY LIFE SERVING IN ITS ARMY[9].
I WAS MARRIED AT THIRTY[10]. A YEAR LATER, MY WIFE GAVE ME SOMETHING I HAD ALWAYS WANTED. A SON.[11]
HIS NAME WAS[12] VLADIMIR. FROM THE FIRST MOMENT HE DREW BREATH[13], HE WAS THE BEST THING IN MY LIFE.
HE GREW INTO[14] A HANDSOME[15] BOY. NO FATHER COULD HAVE BEEN PROUDER[16]. HE WAS TOP[17] IN EVERY CLASS AT SCHOOL, AND A GREAT ATHLETE. ONE DAY HE MIGHT HAVE COMPETED[18] AT OLYMPIC LEVEL[19].
BUT THAT WAS NOT TO BE.[20]
I BELIEVED IT WAS RIGHT[21] FOR VLADIMIR TO SERVE HIS COUNTRY, AS I HAD[22], AND JOIN[23] THE ARMY. HIS MOTHER DISAGREED[24], AND THAT DISAGREEMENT[25] ENDED[26] OUR MARRIAGE.

1. J'aimerais
2. à propos de moi
3. je t'en dirai plus
4. à qui que ce soit
5. Je suis né
6. la Seconde Guerre mondiale
7. tandis que
8. que mon pays passait en premier
9. à servir dans son armée
10. à trente ans
11. Un fils.
12. Il s'appelait
13. Dès son premier souffle
14. En grandissant, il devint
15. beau
16. n'aurait pu être plus fier
17. Il était premier
18. il aurait pu concourir
19. au niveau olympique
20. Mais il n'en a pas eu l'occasion.
21. qu'il était bon
22. comme je l'avais fait
23. qu'il entre dans
24. n'était pas d'accord
25. désaccord
26. mit fin à

1. de partir
2. Je le lui ai ordonné !
3. Il venait d'avoir
4. le combat était rude et difficile
5. Trois semaines après son enrôlement, un sniper
6. un an plus tard
7. veul
8. l'esprit du combat
9. que de perdre
10. je t'ai rencontré
11. de points communs
12. déjà au service de
13. désireux de
14. pour ses convictions
15. aussi loin

YOU ASKED HER TO LEAVE[1]?
I ORDERED HER TO![2]
VLADIMIR JOINED THE ARMY. HE WAS JUST[3] SIXTEEN YEARS OLD.
HE WENT TO AFGHANISTAN, WHERE WE WERE FIGHTING A HARD, DIFFICULT WAR[4].
THREE WEEKS INTO HIS TOUR, A SNIPER[5] SHOT HIM AND HE DIED.
THE WAR ENDED A YEAR LATER[6]. OUR COWARDLY[7] GOVERNMENT LOST THE SPIRIT TO FIGHT[8]. IT HAD ALL BEEN FOR NOTHING!
AND THERE IS NOTHING MORE TERRIBLE THAN FOR A FATHER TO LOSE[9] HIS SON.
...
BUT THEN I MET YOU[10].
ME?
I DON'T UNDERSTAND...
YOU HAVE SO MUCH IN COMMON[11], ALEX. JUST FOURTEEN, AND ALREADY SERVING[12] YOUR COUNTRY! HOW RARE TO FIND A YOUNG PERSON WILLING TO[13] FIGHT FOR THEIR BELIEFS[14]!
I WOULDN'T GO THAT FAR[15]...

YOU HAVE COURAGE.
THE SUGAR FACTORY[1], AND THE CAVE, PROVED THAT[2] EVEN IF[3] YOUR RECORD[4] DID NOT ALREADY[5].
YOU SPEAK MANY LANGUAGES[6].
ONE DAY YOU COULD LEARN[7] RUSSIAN!
YOU RIDE, YOU DIVE, YOU FIGHT[8]!
I HAVE NEVER MET A BOY LIKE YOU ... EXCEPT ONE[9].
I KNOW YOU ARE AN ORPHAN[10], ALEX.
YOU HAVE NO PARENTS ... AND I HAVE NO SON. WE ARE BOTH ALONE.[11]
WE'RE A WORLD APART[12], GENERAL.
WE DON'T NEED TO BE! MY PLAN WILL MAKE THE WORLD A BETTER, STRONGER PLACE. WHEN YOU UNDERSTAND[13] WHAT I'M DOING, YOU WILL SEE WE DO NOT NEED TO BE ENEMIES!
WHAT PLAN? WHAT ARE YOU TALKING ABOUT?
ISN'T IT OBVIOUS[14], ALEX?
I WANT TO ADOPT YOU[15]!

1. La sucrerie

2. l'ont prouvé

3. même si

4. ton historique

5. ne l'avait pas déjà démontré

6. langues

7. apprendre

8. tu combats

9. sauf un

10. que tu es orphelin

11. Nous sommes seuls, tous les deux.

12. Tout nous sépare

13. Lorsque tu auras compris

14. évident

15. t'adopter

LATER THAT NIGHT
THISH WAYYY.[1]
THE BARRACÓN? LOVELY.[2]
YOOOR CELLL[3]. THEE GENERAHL HAS GIVEN YOO[4] SHOMME OF HIS PERSHONAL BOOKSH TO REEEAD[5].
TOLSTOY, DOSTOEVSKY ... TALK ABOUT LIGHT READING[6]. DOESN'T HE HAVE ANY JAMES BOND?
Klang!

1. Par ici.
2. Génial.
3. cellule
4. te donne
5. pour que tu les lises
6. Tu parles d'une lecture distrayante

'NIGHT'[1], CONRAD! I'LL CALL YOU IF I NEED ANYTHING!
Fssh!
FLOODLIGHTS?[2]
OF COURSE. SAROV'S VISITORS HAVE ARRIVED.
AND THERE'S[3] THE RUSSIAN PRESIDENT.
WHATEVER SAROV'S UP TO ...[4] IT'S BEGUN.[5]

1. Bonne nuit

2. Des projecteurs ?

3. voilà

4. Quel que soit le plan de Sarov...

5. il vient de commencer.

1. Réveille-toi, s'il te plaît !

2. Je serai ton escorte

3. aujourd'hui

4. vous voulez dire

5. Comment vous appelez-vous ?

6. Veux-tu prendre ton petit déjeuner ?

7. écuries

8. En réalité

9. jeter un œil sur

10. clôture

11. pour voir

12. un arbre dont je pourrais me servir pour l'escalader

NEXT MORNING
¡DESPIERTA, POR FAVOR![1]
WHO ARE YOU?
SERÉ TU ESCOLTA[2] EL DÍA DE HOY[3].
"ESCORT"? FOLLOWING ME SO I DON'T TRY TO ESCAPE, MORE LIKE[4]. WHAT'S YOUR NAME?
¿COMO SE LLAMA USTED?[5]
JUAN. ¿QUIERES DESAYUNAR?[6]
BREAKFAST? NO ... NO, TAKE ME TO THE STABLES[7]. I WANT TO GO RIDING AGAIN. MONTAR A CABALLO.
ACTUALLY[8] I WANT TO CHECK OUT[9] THAT ELECTRIC FENCE[10], SEE[11] IF THERE'S A TREE I CAN USE TO CLIMB OVER IT[12]...
YAAA!

WELL, SO MUCH FOR[1] THAT IDEA. NOT A[2] TREE IN SIGHT[3].
PELIGRO!
LATER
AND THE DEAD BIRD[4] TELLS ME THOSE "DANGER!" SIGNS[5] OBVIOUSLY AREN'T KIDDING[6]. THAT'S ONE ESCAPE ROUTE[7] I CAN FORGET ABOUT[8].
WHAT ABOUT THE ENTRANCE GATE[9]? TURNER SAID THERE WAS ONLY ONE ROAD INTO THE ESTATE...
THREE ARMED GUARDS, AND THE FENCE GOES ALL THE WAY UP TO[10] THE BARRIER[11]. DOESN'T LOOK PROMISING[12]—
Beep Beep
MALCHIK, PODVINSYA!

1. tant pis pour
2. Pas le moindre
3. en vue
4. l'oiseau mort
5. panneaux
6. ne sont pas une blague
7. plan d'évasion
8. sur lequel je peux tirer un trait
9. grille d'entrée
10. s'étend tout le long, jusqu'à
11. barrière
12. prometteur

HMMM.
COME ON[1], JUAN. LET'S GO HAVE THAT BREAKFAST.
SOON
Splash!
GIGGLE[2]
HELLO, WHAT'S GOING ON[3] AT THE POOL?
GOOD MORNING, ALEX! COME HERE![4]

1. Viens

2. [petits rires]

3. qu'est-ce qui se passe

4. Viens par là !

ALLOW ME TO INTRODUCE[1] MY OLD FRIEND, BORIS KIRIYENKO ... THE PRESIDENT OF RUSSIA.
BORIS, THIS IS THE BOY I WAS TELLING YOU ABOUT[2].
IT IS A PLEASURE.
TY BIL PRAV, ON POKHOZJ NA VLADIMIRA.
SORRY, WHAT?
YOU REMIND HIM OF[3] MY SON.
WOULD YOU LIKE A SWIM, ALEX? TO COOL YOU DOWN[4] AFTER RIDING?
NO THANKS. UNUSUAL LIFEGUARDS[5] YOU HAVE THERE.
SOME COMPANY FOR OUR GUEST. AFTER ALL[6], BORIS IS ON HOLIDAY.
UNFORTUNATELY, WE STILL[7] HAVE WORK TO DO. A LOCAL TV STATION[8] HAS REQUESTED AN INTERVIEW WITH OUR DISTINGUISHED VISITOR[9], AND BORIS HAS AGREED[10].

1. Permets-moi de te présenter

2. dont je te parlais

3. Tu lui rappelles

4. Pour te rafraîchir

5. Drôles de gardes du corps

6. Après tout

7. encore

8. Une chaîne de télévision locale

9. éminent visiteur

10. a accepté

1. les voilà qui arrivent !

2. pour toi tout seul

3. après déjeuner

4. que tu te joindras à nous

5. plat de résistance

6. j'arrive à régler la question de

7. en fait

AH, HERE THEY ARE NOW![1]
YOU CAN HAVE THE POOL TO YOURSELF[2], ALEX. WE'RE GOING INTO SANTIAGO AFTER LUNCH[3], BUT I HOPE YOU'LL JOIN US[4] FOR DINNER. THE CHEF HAS PLANNED A VERY SPECIAL MAIN COURSE[5].
POYEZHAI, BORIS. TAM BUDET BEZUPRECHNO.
GIGGLE
INTO SANTIAGO, EH? THAT COULD BE MY CHANCE...
...IF I CAN DO SOMETHING ABOUT[6] JUAN, THAT IS[7].

LATER
NNNGH!
OW!
¿QUÉ PASA?[1] ¿QUÉ TIENES?[2]
OOOF!
SMACK!
SORRY, JUAN...
...BUT I HAVE TO GET OUT[3] AND TELL SOMEONE WHAT'S REALLY GOING ON AROUND HERE[4].

1. Qu'est-ce qu'il y a ?

2. Qu'est-ce que t'as ?

3. il faut que je sorte

4. par ici

SANTIAGO AFTER LUNCH ... HOPE THEY TAKE ALL OF THE LIMOS[1].
ENTERVYU S PRIZIDENTOM PROSHLO HOROSHO, YA DUMAYU.
!
NEED TO FIND SOMEWHERE TO HIDE[2]...
A-HA!
BRRRR, SERIOUS AIR-CONDITIONING[3]! WHICH PART OF THE HOUSE IS THIS...?

1. limousines

2. où me cacher

3. elle marche fort, la clim

...OH. I HAVEN'T BEEN IN HERE[1] YET[2]!
SOME KIND OF EDITING SUITE[3], LIKE A TV STUDIO ... THEY'RE WATCHING[4] THE WHOLE HOUSE!
BUT THOSE ARE RECORDINGS[5] OF STUFF[6] THAT HAPPENED EARLIER[7] ... WHAT ARE THEY DOING IN HERE?
NO TIME[8] TO THINK ABOUT THAT NOW. I HAVE TO GET OUT AND CONTACT THE CIA!

1. venu ici

2. encore

3. studio de montage

4. Ils surveillent

5. des enregistrements

6. de choses

7. ont déjà eu lieu

8. Je n'ai pas le temps

1. bientôt fini

2. C'est maintenant ou jamais.

3. que l'un d'entre eux

THE GUARDS HAVE GONE, BUT LUNCH WILL BE OVER SOON[1]. IT'S NOW OR NEVER.[2]
I JUST HOPE ONE OF THEM[3] IS OPEN...
KLIK
...BINGO!
AND NOW ... I WAIT.

PHEW!
HOTTER[1] IN HERE THAN I EXPECTED[2]. I HOPE THEY DON'T TAKE TOO LONG[3].
SOMEONE'S COMING, BUT I CAN'T MAKE OUT[4] WHAT THEY'RE SAYING...
Whump
YES! I PICKED[5] A GOOD CAR...
Vrrrrrrrm...
...AND NOW WE'RE MOVING[6]. SO FAR, SO GOOD.[7]
STOPPED AGAIN. MUST BE[8] AT THE GATE.
PLEASE DON'T OPEN THE BOOT[9], YOU DIDN'T CHECK IT[10] ON THAT CAR THIS MORNING...
...MOVING AGAIN! I WONDER HOW FAR IT IS[11] TO SANTIAGO? I'LL HAVE TO LISTEN OUT[12] FOR WHEN WE ARRIVE.
THEN I CAN USE THE CHEWING GUM SMITHERS GAVE ME TO BLOW OPEN[13] THE BOOT...
WAIT[14], WHAT'S HAPPENING?
WE'VE STOPPED AGAIN!

1. Il fait plus chaud

2. que je ne pensais

3. ne vont pas trop tarder

4. je n'arrive pas à distinguer

5. J'ai choisi

6. on roule

7. Jusqu'ici tout va bien.

8. On doit être

9. le coffre

10. tu ne l'as pas contrôlé

11. à quelle distance on est

12. que je guette les bruits

13. pour forcer l'ouverture de

14. Hé

GET OUT.[1]
IF YOU WANTED TO VISIT SANTIAGO, YOU ONLY HAD TO ASK[2]. BUT I DO NOT THINK YOU DID. YOU WERE TRYING TO ESCAPE[3].
OH, NO...
YOU DISAPPOINT ME[4], ALEX. YOU HAVE SEEN THE EXTENT OF MY SECURITY[5].
DID YOU THINK I WOULD ALLOW[6] A CAR TO ENTER OR LEAVE WITHOUT KNOWING EXACTLY WHO AND WHAT IS INSIDE[7]?
DO YOU KNOW WHAT THIS IS[8], ALEX?
NO? THEN WATCH.[9]

1. Sors de là.

2. il suffisait de le demander

3. de t'enfuir

4. Tu me déçois

5. l'étendue de mon système de sécurité

6. que j'autoriserais

7. qui et quoi est à l'intérieur

8. ce que c'est, ça

9. Alors regarde bien.

IT IS A VERY SOPHISTICATED SENSOR[1]. IT DETECTS THE HUMAN HEARTBEAT[2].
Ba-dum...
Ba-dum...
Ba-dum...
EVERY CAR IS SCANNED[3] AT THE BARRIER. WHEN THE GUARD HEARD ONE MORE HEARTBEAT[4] THAN HE SHOULD HAVE, HE KNEW SOMETHING WAS WRONG[5].
Ba-dum...
Ba-dum...
DO YOU NOT REMEMBER WHAT I TOLD YOU? THAT IF YOU TRIED TO ESCAPE, YOU COULD BE SHOT[6]?
CONRAD VERY MUCH WISHES TO[7] SHOOT YOU. HE BELIEVES I AM A FOOL TO KEEP YOU AS MY GUEST.
HE IS RIGHT.[8]
AFTER ALL I HAVE OFFERED YOU[9], YOU MAKE AN ENEMY OF ME. I WANT YOU TO BE MY SON ... BUT YOU FORCE ME TO DESTROY YOU[10].

1. capteur très sophistiqué

2. les battements de cœur humain

3. passée au détecteur

4. a entendu un battement de cœur de trop

5. clochait

6. tu pourrais être exécuté

7. meurt d'envie de

8. Il a raison.

9. Après tout ce que je t'ai offert

10. à t'éliminer

LISTEN TO[1] THE SOUND OF YOUR OWN FEAR[2]! IT BETRAYS YOU![3]
DUMDUMDUMDU..
BHANNG.
AND WHEN YOU HEAR[4] SILENCE - IT COULD BE[5] ANY MOMENT[6], NOW - THAT IS WHEN YOU WILL KNOW[7] YOU ARE DEAD.
HE HAS LEARNED HIS LESSON.[8]
TAKE HIM BACK TO HIS ROOM.
CUBA
HDA 0147

1. Écoute

2. ta propre frayeur

3. Elle te trahit !

4. quand tu entendras

5. ce qui pourrait arriver

6. d'un moment à l'autre

7. alors tu sauras que

8. Il a compris le message.

YOOO ARRE INNNVITED TO DINNNER[1].
LATER THAT EVENING
SORRY, LEFT MY DINNER JACKET[2] IN ENGLAND. ANYWAY[3], I'M NOT HUNGRY.
IT IS NNNOT AN INNNVITATION YOO MAY REFFFUSE[4].
YOOO HAVE FIVE MINNNUTESH. I WILL WAIT OUTSSHIDE[5].
OH, WHAT THE HELL[6].
AT LEAST[7] I MIGHT GET[8] SOME ANSWERS.

1. au dîner

2. j'ai laissé mon smoking

3. De toute façon

4. que tu peux refuser

5. à l'extérieur

6. et puis zut

7. Au moins

8. j'obtiendrai peut-être

ALEX! I'M GLAD[1] YOU'RE HERE. I DIDN'T WANT TO START WITHOUT YOU[2].
COME, SIT AT MY RIGHT HAND[3].
FIRST, CAVIAR IMPORTED[4] DIRECTLY FROM THE BLACK SEA[5].
NO VODKA FOR YOU, THOUGH[6]. YOU ARE TOO YOUNG.
WHAT ABOUT YOU[7], ALEXIE?
I DO NOT DRINK, BORIS. YOU KNOW THAT.
ALL THE MORE FOR US![8] HA!
MY FRIENDS, I HOPE YOU WILL FORGIVE ME[9] FOR SPEAKING IN ENGLISH. OUR GUEST HAS SADLY[10] NOT YET LEARNED[11] OUR GLORIOUS[12] LANGUAGE.

1. Je suis content
2. commencer sans toi
3. à ma droite
4. importé
5. [la mer Noire, située entre l'Ukraine, la Russie, la Géorgie, la Turquie, la Bulgarie et la Roumanie]
6. par contre
7. Et toi
8. Il y en aura plus pour nous !
9. j'espère que vous me pardonnerez
10. malheureusement
11. pas encore appris
12. magnifique

THIS IS FOR ME A NIGHT[1] OF GREAT SIGNIFICANCE[2]. WHAT CAN I TELL YOU ABOUT BORIS NIKITA KIRIYENKO? MY CLOSEST AND DEAREST FRIEND[3] FOR FIFTY[4] YEARS!
I STILL REMEMBER HIM AS A CHILD[5] WHO TEASED[6] ANIMALS, WHO CRIED[7] WHEN THERE WAS A FIGHT[8], AND NEVER TOLD THE TRUTH[9].
IT IS HARD[10] TO BELIEVE THIS IS THE SAME MAN[11] ENTRUSTED WITH[12] THE PRIVILEGE, THE SACRED HONOUR, OF LEADING[13] OUR GREAT COUNTRY IN THESE DIFFICULT TIMES[14].
WELL, BORIS HAS COME HERE FOR A HOLIDAY. I'M SURE HE NEEDS ONE[15] AFTER SO MUCH WORK. AND THAT IS THE TOAST I WISH TO MAKE[16] TONIGHT.
TO BORIS'S HOLIDAY![17] I HOPE IT WILL BE LONGER[18] AND MORE MEMORABLE THAN HE EVER EXPECTED[19].

1. une soirée

2. très importante

3. Mon ami le plus cher et le plus proche

4. depuis cinquante

5. Je garde de lui le souvenir d'un enfant

6. embêtait

7. pleurait

8. une bagarre

9. ne disait jamais la vérité

10. difficile

11. que c'est à ce même homme

12. que l'on a confié

13. de diriger

14. en ces temps difficiles

15. qu'il en a besoin

16. que je souhaite porter

17. Aux vacances de Boris !

18. plus longues

19. qu'il n'aurait jamais imaginé avoir

HA...
HA HA HA! OO VAC VSEGDA YEST STRANNI CHOOVSTVO YUMORA, ALEXEI!
NA ZDAROVIE!
NA ZDOROVIE!
AND NOW IT BEGINS.[1]
WHAT...?
GAKK!
KKK ... HKKK!
!
KKK...

1. C'est maintenant que tout commence.

ALEXIE...!
Krash!
RELAX, ALEX. THEY ARE ONLY UNCONSCIOUS[1], NOT DEAD.
NOT YET[2], ANYWAY.

1. Ils ont simplement perdu connaissance

2. Pas encore

THIRTY MINUTES LATER
OSTOROZJNO!
THAT'S THE BOMB ... ISN'T IT?[1]
GET IN. WE MUST NOT WASTE TIME[2].
...

1. n'est-ce pas ?

2. perdre du temps

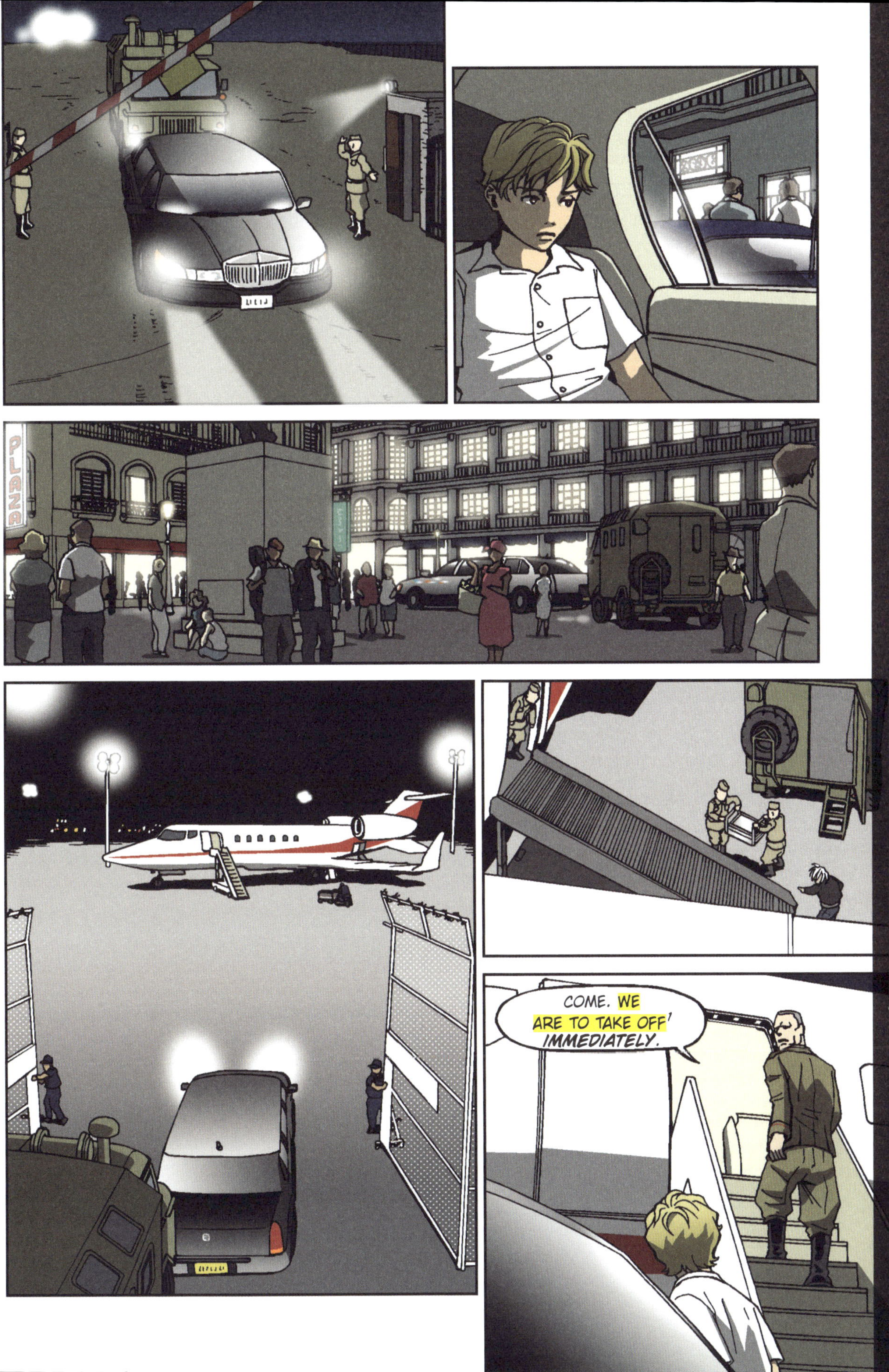
PLAZA
COME. WE ARE TO TAKE OFF[1] IMMEDIATELY.

1. Nous devons décoller

YOU ARE PROBABLY WONDERING[1] WHY I DID NOT KILL YOU EARLIER[2].
IT HAD CROSSED MY MIND[3].
I CAME VERY CLOSE.[4] BUT THEN I THOUGHT ... YOU WERE ONLY DOING[5] YOUR JOB. I ADMIRE THAT.
MY SON VLADIMIR DIED FOR[6] HIS COUNTRY. I AM PROUD[7] THAT YOU WERE PREPARED TO DO THE SAME[8].
...
WHERE ARE WE GOING?
RUSSIA.
MURMANSK[9], TO BE PRECISE - A PORT ON THE KOLA PENINSULA. WE WILL CROSS THE ARCTIC CIRCLE[10], AND MAKE TWO REFUELLING STOPS[11] - ONE IN CANADA, ONE IN EDINBURGH.
YES, EDINBURGH.
YOU WILL BE HOME[12] FOR AN HOUR OR TWO TOMORROW. BUT YOU WILL NOT BE PERMITTED TO[13] LEAVE THE PLANE.
WON'T THE AUTHORITIES WANT TO KNOW WHAT YOU'RE DOING? YOU'RE A COMMUNIST.
THIS IS PRESIDENT KIRIYENKO'S PRIVATE JET[14]. THEY BELIEVE HE IS ON BOARD[15].

1. te demandes probablement

2. tout à l'heure

3. m'a traversé l'esprit

4. Il s'en est fallu de peu.

5. Tu ne faisais que

6. est mort pour

7. fier

8. de même

9. [Mourmansk, port de Russie et base navale, sur la côte nord de la péninsule de Kola]

10. le cercle polaire

11. escales de ravitaillement

12. dans ton pays

13. tu n'auras pas l'autorisation de

14. jet privé

15. à bord

"KIRIYENKO'S PILOT IS FLYING[1]. HE IS LOYAL TO ME, AS ARE MANY RUSSIANS. THEY BELIEVE IN ME, AND THE FUTURE[2] I PROMISE THEM."
YOU STILL HAVEN'T TOLD ME WHAT THAT FUTURE IS.
NO. BUT NOW I WILL TELL YOU, BECAUSE THERE IS NOTHING YOU CAN DO[3] TO STOP IT.
MURMANSK WAS ONCE HOME[4] TO RUSSIA'S NORTHERN FLEET[5] OF SUBMARINES.
BUT RUSSIA'S ARMED FORCES[6] HAVE FALLEN APART[7], JUST LIKE[8] THE REST OF THE COUNTRY. POVERTY[9], CRIME AND CORRUPTION SUCK THE PEOPLE DRY[10].
"MURMANSK IS WHERE THAT DECAY[11] CAN BE SEEN MOST STARKLY[12].
"IT IS NOW HOME TO A FLEET OF ABANDONED[13] SUBMARINES. NUCLEAR SUBMARINES, LEFT TO ROT[14].
"NOBODY CARES.[15] NOBODY WILL FIND THE MONEY[16] TO DO ANYTHING ABOUT THEM.
"BUT THEY CONTAIN ONE-FIFTH[17] OF THE ENTIRE WORLD'S NUCLEAR FUEL[18]! THEY ARE TICKING TIME BOMBS[19] ... AN ACCIDENT WAITING TO HAPPEN[20]."

1. assure le vol

2. à l'avenir

3. tu ne peux rien faire

4. hébergeait autrefois

5. [la flotte du Nord, l'une des quatre flottes principales russes, comptant la moitié des sous-marins russes]

6. forces armées

7. se sont effondrées

8. tout comme

9. La pauvreté

10. saignent le peuple à blanc

11. ce délabrement

12. se voit de la façon la plus frappante

13. laissés à l'abandon

14. qu'on laisse pourrir

15. Tout le monde s'en fiche.

16. ne se soucie de trouver de l'argent

17. un cinquième

18. combustible nucléaire

19. des bombes à retardement

20. prêt à se produire

I HAVE DECIDED TO ARRANGE[1] THAT ACCIDENT.
IF ONE[2] OF THE SUBMARINES BLEW UP[3], IT WOULD BE A CATASTROPHE. A HUGE NUMBER[4] OF RUSSIANS IN THE KOLA PENINSULA AND THE NORTH, AS WELL AS MANY MORE IN NORWAY[5] AND FINLAND, WOULD DIE[6] IMMEDIATELY.
THE FALLOUT[7] WOULD REACH[8] EUROPE, MAKING LONDON UNINHABITABLE[9] FOR MANY YEARS. AND THOUSANDS MORE[10] WOULD FALL ILL[11] AND DIE SLOW, PAINFUL DEATHS[12].
SO WHY DO IT[13]? WHAT WILL IT ACHIEVE?[14]
I AM GIVING THE WORLD A WAKE-UP CALL[15].
TOMORROW NIGHT I WILL PLACE THE BOMB AMONGST THE[16] SUBMARINES.
THE CODES REQUIRED[17] TO DETONATE THE BOMB ARE ENCODED[18] ON THIS KEY CARD[19]. I WILL INSERT IT INTO THE CASING[20], THEN LEAVE.
AT THE TIME[21] OF THE EXPLOSION I WILL BE ON MY WAY TO[22] MOSCOW.
BUT THE SHOCKWAVE[23] WILL BE FELT[24] AROUND THE WHOLE WORLD!

1. d'organiser
2. Si l'un
3. venait à exploser
4. Un nombre incalculable
5. Norvège
6. mourraient
7. Les retombées radioactives
8. attein-draient
9. rendant Londres inhabitable
10. des mil-liers d'autres
11. tom-beraient malades
12. de morts lentes et douloureuses
13. le faire
14. Qu'est-ce que ça apportera ?
15. un coup de semonce
16. au milieu des
17. néces-saires
18. encodés
19. carte magnétique
20. le boîtier
21. Au moment
22. en route pour
23. l'onde de choc
24. ressentie

IMAGINE THE OUTRAGE[1] IT WILL CREATE[2]! THEY WILL ASSUME[3] ONE OF THE SUBMARINES FINALLY COLLAPSED[4]. NOBODY WILL SUSPECT THE TRUTH[5].
YES, THEY WILL![6] THE CIA KNOWS YOU BOUGHT URANIUM! THEY'LL FIND OUT[7] THEIR AGENTS ARE DEAD—
NOBODY WILL BELIEVE THE CIA. NOBODY EVER DOES.[8] ANYWAY, IT WILL BE TOO LATE[9].
INSTEAD[10], THE WORLD WILL UNITE TO CONDEMN[11] RUSSIA OVER[12] THE DISASTER. WE WILL BE HATED[13]. THE RUSSIAN PEOPLE WILL BE ASHAMED[14].
"IF ONLY[15] WE HAD BEEN LESS CARELESS[16], LESS POOR, LESS CORRUPT[17]. IF ONLY WE WERE STILL THE SUPERPOWER[18] WE HAD ONCE BEEN..."
EVERYONE WILL LOOK TO[19] BORIS KIRIYENKO, THE RUSSIAN PRESIDENT, FOR LEADERSHIP[20]. AND WHAT WILL THEY SEE?
THE EDITING SUITE!
YOU INTERVIEWED HIM[21], FILMED HIM...
YES, ALEX. NOW[22] YOU ARE THINKING LIKE A RUSSIAN.

1. l'indignation
2. suscitera
3. Ils penseront que
4. a finalement rendu l'âme
5. la vérité
6. Bien sûr que si !
7. Ils vont apprendre que
8. Personne ne la croit jamais.
9. trop tard
10. Au lieu de cela
11. condamnera unanimement
12. pour avoir causé
13. détestés
14. seront couverts de honte
15. Si seulement
16. moins négligents
17. corrompus
18. superpuissance
19. Tous les regards se tourneront vers
20. pour qu'il agisse en dirigeant
21. Vous l'avez interviewé
22. Ça y est,

1. Nous diffuserons
2. ivre
3. en train de jouer
4. à moitié nues
5. assez jeunes
6. ses filles
7. une grève de train
8. à moitié ivre
9. il a répondu
10. trop pris
11. pour m'occuper de
12. modifierons
13. en ce qui concerne
14. verra que
15. n'est qu'un ivrogne stupide
16. rejettera la responsabilité sur lui
17. Comment a-t-on pu permettre qu'elle devienne
18. qu'on laisse rouiller
19. une décharge nucléaire mortelle
20. la vie était meilleure
21. leur colère
22. éclatera
23. Rien ne pourra l'arrêter.
24. je l'exploiterai

WE WILL RELEASE[1] FILM THAT SHOWS HIM DRUNK[2] BESIDE THE SWIMMING POOL, PLAYING[3] WITH HALF-NAKED[4] GIRLS YOUNG ENOUGH[5] TO BE HIS DAUGHTERS[6]. AND THEN THE INTERVIEW...
"OUR INTERVIEWER ASKED HIM ABOUT A TRAIN STRIKE[7] IN MOSCOW. BORIS WAS ALREADY HALF DRUNK[8], AND REPLIED[9]:"
THIS IS MY HOLIDAY. I'M TOO BUSY[10] TO DEAL WITH[11] THAT.
"BUT WE WILL CHANGE[12] THE QUESTION."
WHAT ARE YOU GOING TO DO ABOUT[13] THE ACCIDENT IN MURMANSK, MR PRESIDENT?
THIS IS MY HOLIDAY. I'M TOO BUSY TO DEAL WITH THAT.
RUSSIA WILL SEE[14] KIRIYENKO FOR THE DRUNKEN IMBECILE HE IS[15], AND BLAME HIM[16].
"THE NORTHERN FLEET WAS ONCE THE PRIDE OF RUSSIA! HOW COULD IT HAVE BEEN ALLOWED TO BECOME[17] A RUSTING[18], LETHAL NUCLEAR DUMP[19]?"
MANY RUSSIANS BELIEVE LIFE WAS BETTER[20] IN THE OLD DAYS. THEY HATE WHAT RUSSIA HAS BECOME. NOW THEIR ANGER[21] WILL BE HEARD[22]. IT WILL BE UNSTOPPABLE.[23]
AND I WILL HARNESS IT[24]!

BEFORE THE NUCLEAR DUST CLOUD[1] HAS SETTLED[2], I WILL HAVE TOTAL CONTROL OF MY COUNTRY! I WILL REBUILD[3] THE BERLIN WALL! START[4] WARS, MANY WARS!
I WILL NOT REST[5] UNTIL COMMUNIST GOVERNMENT IS THE SINGLE DOMINANT POWER[6] IN THE WORLD!
BUT YOU'LL KILL MILLIONS OF YOUR OWN PEOPLE!
PAH! MILLIONS ARE ALREADY DYING IN RUSSIA JUST BECAUSE THEY CANNOT AFFORD[7] FOOD OR MEDICINE!
...
AND WHAT HAPPENS TO ME?[8]
I'VE ALREADY TOLD YOU. YOU WILL BE WITH ME IN MOSCOW. DON'T YOU SEE, ALEX? YOU WILL NOT JUST[9] BE MY SON. YOU WILL HAVE POWER[10]!
YOU WILL BE ONE OF THE MOST POWERFUL PEOPLE IN THE WORLD!
...

1. le nuage de poussière atomique

2. se soit stabilisé

3. reconstruirai

4. Je déclencherai

5. Je n'aurai de cesse

6. le seul pouvoir dominant

7. n'ont pas les moyens d'acheter

8. Et moi dans tout ça ?

9. simplement

10. le pouvoir

1. Tour de contrôle

2. vous avez l'autorisation d'atterrir

3. ravitaillement de routine

4. formalités administratives à bord

5. nous amorçons l'approche finale

6. Pas un mot.

7. que tu es sur le point de

8. de stupide

9. il fera feu

10. simplement endormi

11. camion

TOWER[1] TO RF-1, YOU ARE CLEARED TO LAND[2] FOR ROUTINE REFUELLING[3] ONLY. PLEASE BE PREPARED FOR ADMINISTRATIVE BOARDING[4].
ROGER, TOWER. COMMENCING FINAL APPROACH[5].
EDINBURGH, SCOTLAND, NEXT DAY
YOU WILL NOT SPEAK, ALEX. NOT ONE SINGLE WORD.[6]
CONRAD?
IF CONRAD EVEN THINKS YOU ARE ABOUT TO[7] TRY SOMETHING FOOLISH[8], HE WILL FIRE[9]. DEATH WILL BE INSTANT, BUT IT WILL APPEAR AS IF YOU HAVE MERELY FALLEN ASLEEP[10].
HERE COMES THE REFUELLING TRUCK[11]. REMEMBER, NOW. NOT A SOUND.

D'YE SPEAK ENGLISH? I'VE GOT SOME PAPERS FOR YE TO SIGN[1].
YES.
CHEERS.[2] HERE'S YER RECEIPT[3]. WE'LL HAVE YE BACK IN THE AIR IN NAE TIME AT ALL[4].
THANK YOU.
WILL YE NOT COME OUT AND STRETCH YER LEGS[5]? IT'S A FINE DAY[6], AND WE'VE GOT TEA[7] AND SHORTBREAD[8] IN THE OFFICE.
NO, THANK YOU. WE ARE ALL A LITTLE TIRED.
ALL RIGHT, IF YE'RE SURE. CHEERIO![9]
!
SHHIDOWNN![10]
RELAX, CONRAD. I'M NOT GOING ANYWHERE. MY LEGS ARE A BIT NUMB[11], THAT'S ALL.
Klik - Klik - Klik

1. à vous faire signer

2. Merci.

3. reçu

4. en un rien de temps

5. pour vous dégourdir les jambes

6. une belle journée

7. du thé

8. [biscuits sablés au beurre, spécialité écossaise]

9. Au revoir !

10. Assieds-toi !

11. un peu engourdies

1. Nulle part.

2. mascotte porte-bonheur

3. mal à la tête

4. prendre l'air

5. Tu ne dois pas

6. à ta place

WHERE ARE YOU GOING, ALEX?
NOWHERE.[1]
WHAT'S THAT YOU HAVE IN YOUR HAND?
IT'S MY LUCKY MASCOT[2]. MICHAEL OWEN.
Klik - Kliik
SIT DOWN.
I'VE GOT A HEADACHE[3]. I JUST WANT SOME FRESH AIR[4].
YOU ARE NOT TO[5] LEAVE THE PLANE.
I'M NOT GOING ANYWHERE.
ALEX! RETURN TO YOUR SEAT[6]!
CONRAD...!

BANG!
OOF!

HEY! WHAT D'YE THINK YE'RE DOING?[1]
STRETCHING[2] MY LEGS!
Mmmph!
LOCKED![3]
ONE OF THE DOORS HAS TO BE[4] OPEN, PLEASE...
EXIT
YES!
NOW ALL I NEED IS...[5]
...A PHONE!

1. Qu'est-ce qui te prend ?

2. Je me dégourdis

3. Verrouillée !

4. doit bien être

5. Tout ce qu'il me faut, c'est...

999 WILL HAVE TO DO.[1]
YOU HAVE RUNG[2] THE EMERGENCY SERVICES[3]. WHICH SERVICE DO YOU REQUIRE[4]?
POLICE!
CONNECTING YOU NOW...
SLAM!
WHAT ARE YE DOING HERE, LADDIE[5]?
I NEED TO MAKE A PHONE CALL! IT'S URGENT!
THIS ISNAE[6] A PUBLIC PHONE BOX[7]. THIS ISNAE EVEN A PUBLIC OFFICE[8]. YE[9] SHOULDNAE[10] BE IN HERE.
YOU DON'T UNDERSTAND. THIS IS AN EMERGENCY[11]! JUST LET ME MAKE THE CALL[12]!

1. Je devrai me contenter du 999 [numéro d'urgence].

2. Vous êtes en relation avec

3. police secours

4. demandez-vous

5. p'tit gars

6. Ce n'est pas

7. cabine téléphonique

8. un bureau accessible au public

9. Tu

10. ne devrais pas

11. urgence

12. passer cet appel

YE'RE NOT DOING ANYTHING UNTIL YE TELL ME[1] WHAT'S GOING ON HERE! THIS IS A PRIVATE OFFICE!
LOOK[2], I'M SORRY, BUT I JUST GOT OFF[3] A PLANE A FEW MINUTES AGO[4], AND—
OH, DID YE NOW? WHERE'S YER[5] PASSPORT?
WHAT? I DON'T HAVE—
WELL, THAT'S A VERY SERIOUS MATTER[6], LADDIE. YE CANNAE[7] ENTER THE COUNTRY WITHOUT A PASSPORT.
ALL RIGHT, LOOK...
I KNOW THIS IS HARD TO BELIEVE[8], BUT I WORK FOR THE GOVERNMENT. JUST LET ME CALL THEM, THEY'LL PROVE IT! I'M A SPY—
A SPY?! HOW OLD ARE YE?[9]
...FOURTEEN.
Ho-ho!
I THINK YE'VE BEEN WATCHING TOO MUCH[10] TELEVISION, LADDIE!
IT'S TRUE! THERE'S A MAN IN A PLANE ON THE RUNWAY[11] AND UNLESS[12] I MAKE THIS CALL, HE'S GOING TO KILL A LOT OF PEOPLE!

1. jusqu'à ce que tu m'aies dit

2. Écoutez

3. je viens de descendre de

4. il y a quelques minutes

5. ton

6. c'est très grave

7. Tu ne peux pas

8. vous aurez du mal à le croire

9. Quel âge as-tu ?

10. tu as trop regardé

11. sur la piste

12. à moins que

THE ONLY THING YE'RE DOING IS COMING WITH ME TO SECURITY. COME ALONG NOW![1]
FOR GOD'S SAKE[2], HE'S GOT A NUCLEAR BOMB! HE'S GOING TO DETONATE IT[3] IN MURMANSK! YOU HAVE TO LET ME CALL MI6!
AH, ALEX! THERE YOU ARE![4]
WHO ARE YE?
I AM ALEX'S FATHER. ISN'T THAT RIGHT, ALEX?
HE'LL KILL THE GUARD IF I DENY IT[5]...
YES ... DAD.
HAS ALEX MADE A TELEPHONE CALL?
NO. WEE RASCAL[6] WAS HELPING HIMSELF[7] WHEN I CAUGHT HIM[8], AND I PUT A STOP TAE IT[9].
SO WHAT'S ALL THIS BUSINESS[10] ABOUT BOMBS AND SPIES?

1. Allez, suis-moi !

2. Bon sang

3. la faire exploser

4. Te voilà !

5. si je nie

6. Ce petit chenapan

7. allait téléphoner

8. je l'ai attrapé

9. je l'en ai empêché

10. toute cette histoire

1. débordante

2. dernièrement

3. Je vais le ramener

4. les éléments dont vous avez besoin

5. Vous n'allez plus jamais être ennuyé

6. Dépêche-toi

7. rendez-vous

ALEX HAS AN OVERACTIVE[1] IMAGINATION, AND SOME MENTAL PROBLEMS. HE HAS NOT BEEN WELL LATELY[2].
I WILL RETURN HIM[3] TO THE PLANE. MY ASSISTANT WILL GIVE YOU ALL THE DETAILS YOU REQUIRE[4].
WELL ... ALL RIGHT, THEN. BUT KEEP HIM OUT OF TROUBLE!
OH, DO NOT WORRY.
YOU WILL NEVER BE TROUBLED AGAIN[5], I PROMISE. CONRAD?
Blam!
HURRY UP[6], ALEX. WE HAVE A DATE[7] WITH A BOMB.

MURMANSK, RUSSIA
WELCOME[1] TO THE *FUTURE*, ALEX.
LOVELY. IS THIS AIRPORT EVEN IN *USE*[2]?
ONLY BY *US*.[3] COME! OUR *DESTINY* AWAITS[4].
BOMBA V YCHASTOK GROOZ. PREENYESEETYE MNYE.
DA, GYENERAL.
VHODITYE.

1. Bienvenue

2. en service

3. Pour nous uniquement.

4. nous attend

DO THEY REALLY KEEP NUCLEAR SUBS[1] IN HERE? I'VE SEEN BETTER SECURITY[2] IN A SUPERMARKET CAR PARK[3]!
EY! KTO ETO? SHTO VHI ZDES DELAYETYE?

1. sous-marins

2. une sécurité plus renforcée

3. parking

Blam! Blam!
THERE IT IS ... THE BASE OF THE NORTHERN FLEET. WHAT A DUMP![1]

1. Quel dépotoir !

Brakka Brakka Brakka
POMOGITYE!
SPASAITYE NAS!
BrakkaBrakka
!
THEY'RE KILLING ALL THE STAFF[1]!
AAARGH!
Blam!
Blam!

1. le personnel

BOOM!
VHODITYE E UVAZHAYEMIY!
COME, ALEX.
WHERE ARE THEY ALL GOING?
TO THEIR POSITIONS.[1] ANY COUNTER-ATTACK[2] WILL FIND[3] THE BAY[4] VERY WELL DEFENDED.
NOW LOOK!

1. Ils prennent leurs positions.

2. S'il y a une contre-attaque

3. ils découvriront

4. que la baie est

OH...
...WOW.

FFOLLOW ME.
HEY, **WATCH IT!**[1] THESE THINGS ARE **TIGHT**[2]!
THAT PAAAIN WILL **ENNND** SOON ENNNOUGH.
VERY GOOD. NOW **STAND BACK**[3]!
Beep
AND SO[4] ... ALEX.

1. atten-tion !

2. serrés

3. recule

4. Bon, ben

YOU ARE STANDING[1] IN THE NUCLEAR SUBMARINE REPAIR SHIPYARD[2] OF MURMANSK. GROUND ZERO[3] OF MY NEW WORLD.
BUT I REGRET I CANNOT STAY[4] WITH YOU ANY LONGER[5].
CONRAD WILL POSITION[6] THE BOMB ON THE SUBMARINE, DIRECTLY OVER[7] THE NUCLEAR REACTOR[8].
I, OF COURSE, MUST MAKE MY WAY TO MOSCOW. ALONE.
YOU WILL BE VAPORIZED INSTANTLY[9], BEFORE YOUR BRAIN[10] EVEN UNDERSTANDS WHAT IS HAPPENING.
CONRAD IS VERY DISAPPOINTED. HE STILL[11] WANTED TO KILL YOU HIMSELF[12].
IN THE END[13], YOU WERE MORE STUPID THAN I THOUGHT[14]. I SHOULD HAVE EXPECTED IT. A WESTERN[15] CHILD, EDUCATED[16] IN ENGLAND...
WHY COULDN'T YOU SEE[17] WHAT I WAS OFFERING YOU[18]? YOU COULD HAVE BEEN MY SON ... BUT YOU CHOSE[19] TO BE MY ENEMY.
GOODBYE, ALEX.

1. Tu te trouves

2. le chantier naval où étaient entretenus les sous-marins nucléaires

3. [nom attribué au site des tours jumelles de New York, après les attentats du 11 septembre 2001]

4. de ne pouvoir rester

5. plus longtemps

6. placera

7. au-dessus de

8. réacteur

9. instantanément désintégré

10. cerveau

11. quand même

12. lui-même

13. En fin de compte

14. que je ne pensais

15. occidental

16. élevé

17. cerner

18. je t'offrais

19. tu as choisi

I HAVE A JOBBB TO DO ... BUT THEN[1] I THINNK YOO ANND I WILLL HAVE SHOME TIME TOOGETHER[2]. ANND YOOO WILL[3] SHHUFFER.
JUST TALKING TO YOU[4] MAKES ME SUFFER, FRANKENSTEIN.
Zmmmmmm...
THE CRANE'S[5] A HUGE ELECTROMAGNET[6].
Klunk!
THAT'S HOW[7] HE'S GOING TO POSITION THE BOMB!
Zmmmmmmm...
NOW OR NEVER, ALEX, BECAUSE THIS WOULD BE A RUBBISH PLACE[8] TO DIE...
Bzzzzhhh...

1. ensuite
2. qu'on va passer un moment ensemble
3. tu vas
4. Le simple fait de te parler
5. La grue est
6. électro-aimant
7. comme ça qu'
8. un endroit pourri

1. Mâche
2. pendant
3. Je suis confronté à la mort
4. Un vrai gosse occidental !

CHEW[1] THE GUM FOR[2] THIRTY SECONDS, THAT'S WHAT SMITHERS SAID...
IF SAROV COULD SEE THIS ... FACING DEATH[3], AND I'M CHEWING
GUM. "TYPICAL WESTERN KID"![4]
YUCK.[5]
NEED TO WORK ON[6] THAT FLAVOUR[7], SMITHERS...
...LET'S HOPE THE OTHER PART OF THE FORMULA[8] WORKS BETTER[9].

5. Beurk.
6. retravailler
7. saveur
8. formule
9. fonctionne mieux

Krak!
OWW!
HHEYYY!
Zmmmmm...
TIME FORRR' THAT SHUFFERING!
Thud!
!!

1. C'est l'heure de

MMMF!
TOOO SHLOWW[1].
SLAP!
Unh!
FFOOLISHH BOY! YOOO THOUGHT...
Brakka Brakka Brakka
...WHAT?

1. lent

Brakka Brakka
AN ATTAAACK? BUT HOW—
BooM!
KLANG!
IS THAT AAALL YOOO'VE GOT?[1]
Vrmmmmmm
Krash
mmm...
Blam!
Brakka Brakka
Brakka Brakka B
Blam!
Blam!

1. C'est tout ce que tu as ?

WHUD!
THWAK!
Aaah!
Brakka
Brakka
BOOM
Brakka
Brakka
Brakka
UKK.

CAN'T ... BREATHE[1] ... BLACKING OUT[2]...
WAIT...
WHAT'S THAT...?
THE DISC[3]...
SAROV SAID ... METAL PINS[4]...
ALL ... OVER ...[5] CONRAD'S BODY...
MMMF!
WHA...?
TOOK ME[6] BYY SURRRPRISE ... WON'T DOO THAT AGAINNN![7]
I DON'T NEED TO.

1. respirer

2. Je m'évanouis

3. Ce disque

4. des broches métalliques

5. partout... dans...

6. Tu m'as eu

7. Tu ne le referas plus !

WHAAAT...?
!
AAAAAAAAAAAA
Snap!
KLANG!

WHAT AN ATTRACTIVE SIGHT[1].
Wuppa Wuppa
Budda Budda Budda
Wuppa
Wuppa wuppa...
BOOM
FEELS LIKE I'VE GONE TEN ROUNDS[2] WITH A HEAVYWEIGHT[3]. BUT I'LL FEEL WORSE[4] IF THAT BOMB GOES OFF[5]...
THE CONTROLS[6] SEEM PRETTY[7] SIMPLE...
Zmmmmm...
GOT IT![8]

1. beau spectacle

2. j'avais subi dix rounds

3. boxeur poids-lourd

4. je me sentirai encore moins bien

5. se déclenche

6. Les commandes

7. assez

8. Je l'ai !

1. que je me débarrasse de

2. poids encombrant

NOW I NEED TO DITCH[1] THIS EXCESS WEIGHT[2]!
klik
Splash!
Brakka Brakka
WOAH!
Sptang!
Sptang!
Sptang!
Budda Budda Budda
THANKS, HELICOPTER GUY!

Zmmmmmm...
Klang!
Zmmmmmm...
CAN'T THIS THING GO ANY FASTER[1]...?!
GOT IT. NOW TO LOWER IT SLOWLY[2] ... CAREFULLY...
Klang
BOOM!

1. un peu plus vite

2. le faire descendre lentement

PHEW![1] JUST A GRENADE GOING OFF[2]. I THOUGHT I WAS A GONER[3]...!
THERE'S THE CARD!
Beeeep
THE COUNTDOWN[4]'S STOPPED. I DID IT![5]
I DID IT!
PUT IT BACK.[6]

1. Pfft !

2. qui a éclaté

3. que j'étais fichu

4. compte à rebours

5. J'ai réussi !

6. Remets-la.

IT'S OVER[1], GENERAL.
CONRAD'S DEAD, AND THE RUSSIAN ARMY'S HERE. SOMEONE MUST HAVE TIPPED THEM OFF[2].
I CAN STILL[3] DETONATE THE BOMB WITH AN OVERRIDE[4]. I WILL DIE WITH YOU, BUT THE RESULT WILL BE THE SAME.
WHAT? YOUR "BETTER WORLD[5]"?
IT'S ALL I EVER WANTED[6], ALEX. I WAS ONLY DOING WHAT I BELIEVED IN[7].
NOW GIVE ME THE CARD, OR I WILL SHOOT YOU[8].
NOOOOO!
GUESS YOU'D BETTER SHOOT ME.[9]
BUT WHY...?

1. C'est fini

2. a dû les renseigner

3. encore

4. un système d'annulation

5. monde meilleur

6. C'était tout ce que je voulais

7. ce en quoi je croyais

8. ou je tire

9. Il vaudrait mieux que vous me tiriez dessus.

1. je préfère mourir

2. comme vous

3. Soit.

BECAUSE I'D RATHER BE DEAD[1] THAN HAVE A FATHER LIKE YOU[2].
SO BE IT.[3]
GOODBYE, ALEX.
FOR EVER.
BLAM...

LONDON
WE'VE LOST[1] ALEX RIDER.
SORRY, ALAN. I KNOW IT'S NOT WHAT YOU WANTED TO HEAR[2], BUT THAT'S THE END OF IT[3].
MMM.
HE DID VERY WELL.[4]
OH, YES. I HAD AN EMAIL FROM JOE BYRNE AT THE CIA. HE WAS UPSET[5] ABOUT THE LOSS OF HIS OWN AGENTS[6], BUT HE WAS FULL OF PRAISE[7] FOR[8] ALEX.
HE DEFINITELY OWES US[9] A FAVOUR.
IT WOULDN'T SURPRISE ME IF THE CIA STARTED TRAINING[10] THEIR OWN TEENAGE SPY[11] NOW. THEY'RE ALWAYS COPYING OUR IDEAS.
WHEN WE'RE NOT COPYING THEIRS[12].
I'VE READ THE FILE[13], BUT PERHAPS YOU CAN FILL ME IN[14] ON THE DETAILS. HOW EXACTLY DID THE RUSSIANS FIND OUT ABOUT SAROV IN TIME[15]?

1. perdu

2. ce que tu voulais entendre

3. c'est comme ça, un point c'est tout

4. Il a été remarquable.

5. bouleversé

6. ses propres agents

7. il a été très élogieux

8. à l'égard d'

9. Il nous doit vraiment

10. à former

11. leur propre ado espion

12. les leurs

13. dossier

14. me mettre au courant

15. à temps

1. ce qui s'est passé
2. il est tombé sur
3. à propos de lui
4. ne l'a pas cru
5. les a retrouvés
6. a tiré sur
7. tout était fichu
8. heureusement
9. fonctionnait
10. a tout entendu
11. non plus
12. une balle dans la tête
13. ont lancé un assaut sur le chantier
14. des forces navales
15. des navires de guerre

BECAUSE OF WHAT HAPPENED[1] AT EDINBURGH AIRPORT. ALEX ESCAPED FROM SAROV'S PLANE AND RAN INTO[2] A SECURITY GUARD.
ALEX ACTUALLY TOLD HIM THE TRUTH ABOUT HIMSELF[3], ABOUT US, EVERYTHING. BUT THE GUARD DIDN'T BELIEVE IT[4].
"SAROV CAUGHT UP WITH THEM[5] AND SHOT[6] THE GUARD. ALEX MUST HAVE THOUGHT THAT WAS THE END OF IT[7]...
"...BUT LUCKILY[8] FOR US, THE GUARD'S RADIO WAS ACTIVATED[9] THE WHOLE TIME. HIS OFFICE HEARD EVERYTHING[10]."
THEY DIDN'T BELIEVE IT EITHER[11], OF COURSE ... UNTIL THEY FOUND HIM WITH A BULLET IN HIS HEAD[12]. THEN THEY CALLED US.
I CONTACTED MURMANSK, AND THE RUSSIANS STORMED THE YARD[13] WITH A NAVAL FORCE[14] AND GUNSHIPS[15].
WHAT HAPPENED TO THE NUCLEAR BOMB?

MMM. WHERE *IS* THE PRESIDENT?
THEY FOUND HIM **LOCKED UP**[5] ON SKELETON KEY, SHOUTING HIS HEAD OFF[6] AND BLAMING[7] EVERYONE **EXCEPT**[8] HIMSELF. HE'S BACK[9] IN MOSCOW NOW.
THE ***RUSSIANS*** HAVE IT. APPARENTLY IT WAS POWERFUL ENOUGH[1] TO ***KILL*** EVERYONE ON THE KOLA PENINSULA AND ***CONTAMINATE*** MOST[2] OF EUROPE.
IT REALLY ***WOULD*** HAVE FORCED KIRIYENKO OUT OF POWER[3]. NOBODY ***LIKES*** HIM MUCH[4] ANYWAY.
AND WHAT DO THE ***CUBANS*** HAVE TO SAY FOR THEMSELVES[10]?
THEY'VE ***DISOWNED***[11] SAROV. NOTHING TO DO[12] WITH THEM, THEY HAD NO IDEA WHAT HE WAS PLANNING, ***BLAH BLAH***[13].
RIGHT, AND ***I'M*** THE ***PRIME MINISTER***[14]. STILL[15], IF NOT FOR ALEX[16]...
...WHO ***KNOWS*** WHAT MIGHT HAVE HAPPENED.
WHERE *IS* ALEX NOW?

1. assez puissante
2. une grande partie
3. à renoncer au pouvoir
4. ne l'apprécie beaucoup
5. enfermé
6. hurlant à tue-tête
7. en rejetant la faute sur
8. sauf
9. Il est de retour
10. donnent comme explications
11. désavoué
12. Tout ça n'a rien à voir
13. etc. etc.
14. moi, je suis le Premier ministre
15. Tout de même
16. si Alex n'avait pas été là

1. essaie au moins
2. à peine
3. que tu es rentré
4. aller voir
5. Je vois bien que
6. Je vais bien
7. aller au cinéma
8. aller marcher
9. Je viens
10. très bien tout seul

PLEASE, ALEX, AT LEAST TRY[1] TO EAT. YOU'VE HARDLY[2] TOUCHED ANYTHING SINCE YOU GOT BACK[3].
CHELSEA, LONDON
I THINK YOU SHOULD GO SEE[4] A DOCTOR. IT'S OBVIOUS[5] YOU'RE NOT WELL.
NO.
I'M FINE.[6]
WELL THEN, WHAT DO YOU WANT TO DO TODAY? YOU WANT TO GO CATCH A MOVIE[7]?
I THINK I'LL JUST GO FOR A WALK[8].
ALL RIGHT. I'LL COME[9] WITH YOU.
NO. THANKS, JACK, REALLY. BUT I'M FINE ON MY OWN[10].
Slam

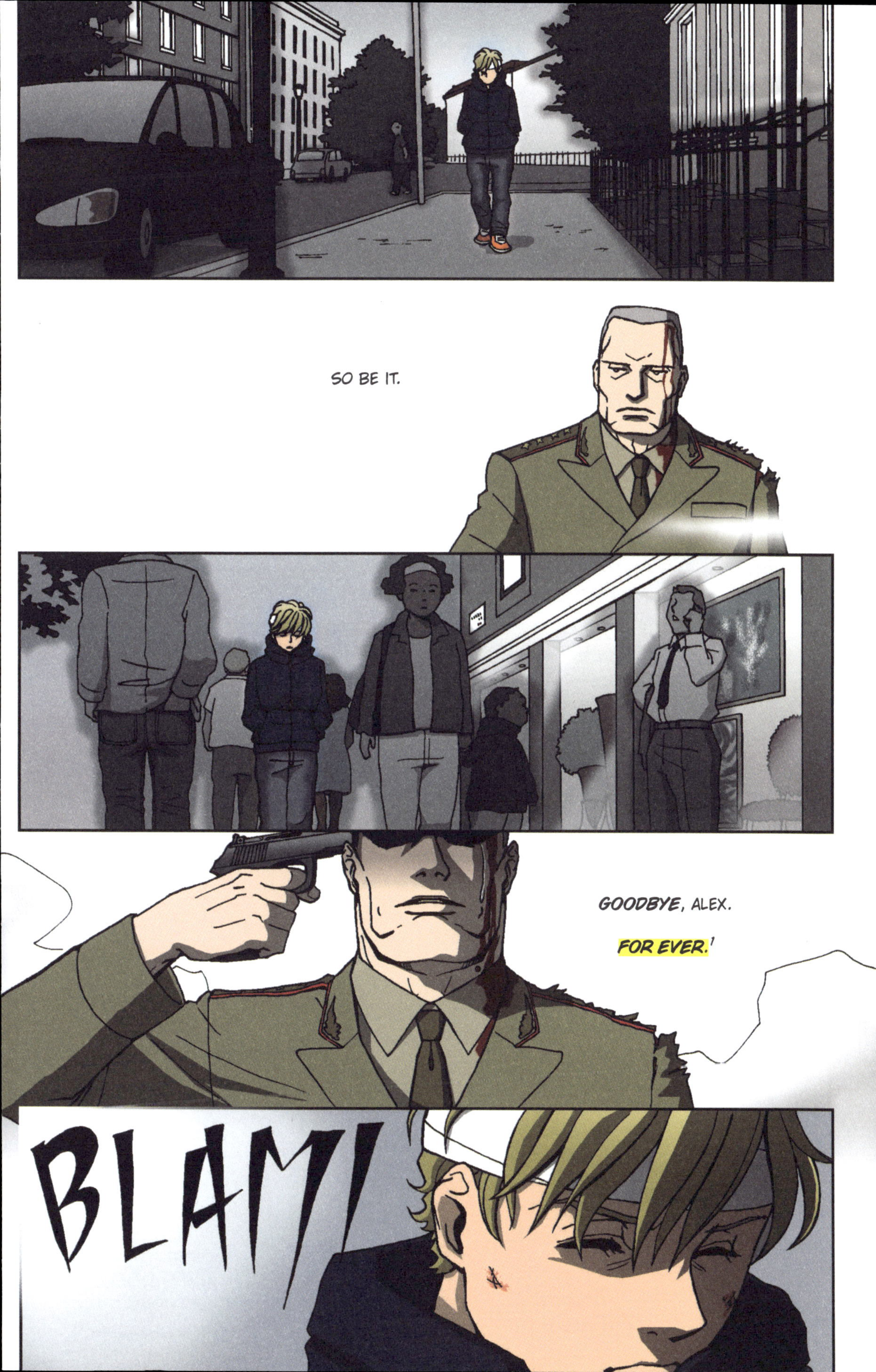
SO BE IT.
GOODBYE, ALEX.
FOR EVER.[1]
BLAM!

1. Pour toujours.

1. inquiète

2. ils n'ont pas voulu me dire

3. de bleus

4. tu m'as envoyé un texto

5. J'ai vu

6. se suicider

7. il s'est tiré une balle

8. juste

9. c'était de ma faute

ALEX!
ARE YOU ALL RIGHT? I WAS SO **WORRIED**[1], THEY WOULDN'T TELL ME[2] WHERE THEY **TOOK** YOU...
WHAT HAPPENED? YOU'RE **COVERED** IN BRUISES[3].
I CAN'T **TELL** YOU, SAB. YOU **KNOW** THAT.
WELL, IF YOU **DON'T** WANT TO TALK ABOUT IT, WHY DID YOU **TEXT** ME[4]?
I ... I JUST WANTED TO **SEE** YOU.
I WATCHED[5] A MAN **KILL HIMSELF**[6] LAST WEEK. HE ... HE JUST SHOT HIMSELF[7], RIGHT[8] IN **FRONT** OF ME.
AND ... IT WAS **MY FAULT**[9].

I DON'T BELIEVE THAT.
BUT IT'S TRUE. IT WAS ALL SO UNREAL[1]...
BUT THIS WAS THE LAST TIME[2].
OH, YOU ALWAYS SAY THAT.
I MEAN IT.[3]
I JUST WANT A NORMAL LIFE, SAB. AS NORMAL AS MINE CAN BE[4], ANYWAY.
DO YOU FANCY[5] COMING TO FRANCE, THEN?
WHAT?
WELL, CORNWALL WAS RUINED[6], WASN'T IT? BUT MY PARENTS ARE TAKING ME[7] TO THE SOUTH[8] OF FRANCE NEXT MONTH[9], SO I WANT YOU TO COME WITH US.

1. si irréel

2. là, c'était la dernière fois

3. Je suis sérieux.

4. aussi normale que possible

5. Ça te dit de

6. c'était raté

7. m'emmènent

8. sud

9. le mois prochain

1. Cela ne dérange pas tes parents ?

2. t'aiment bien

3. emprunter

4. rien de prétentieux

5. écuries

6. Tu sembles vraiment

7. avoir besoin de

8. repos

9. éloigne-toi de tout... ça

10. depuis des semaines

11. Je meurs de faim.

DON'T YOUR PARENTS MIND?[1]
THEY LIKE YOU[2], ALEX. WE'RE JUST GOING TO BORROW[3] A FRIEND'S HOUSE, IT'S NOTHING FANCY[4].
WELL, APART FROM THE SWIMMING POOL. AND THE MARINA. AND THE STABLES[5]...
A REAL FAMILY HOLIDAY...
YOU DO LOOK[6] LIKE YOU NEED[7] A REST[8], ALEX. COME WITH US AND GET AWAY FROM ALL ... THIS[9].
THAT'S THE BEST IDEA I'VE HEARD IN WEEKS[10].
COME ON, LET'S GET SOMETHING TO EAT. I'M STARVING.[11]
THE END

Graphic Novelisation by Antony Johnston
Illustrated by Kanako and Yuzuru

Published by arrangement with Walker Books Limited, London.
87 Vauxhall Walk, London SE11 5HJ
www.walker.co.uk

21, rue du Montparnasse
75283 Paris Cedex 06

HARRAP's® est une marque de Larousse SAS.
www.harrap.com

ISBN 978 2 81 870350 2

Direction de la publication : Carine Girac-Marinier
Direction éditoriale : Claude Nimmo
Notes en marge : Patricia Seixas
Révision des notes : Giovanni Picci
Relecture : Élisabeth Le Saux
Informatique éditoriale : Philippe Cazabet, Marie-Noëlle Tilliette
Fabrication : Rebecca Dubois
Remerciements à Marie Gabiache

ANTHONY HOROWITZ (BA/Nielsen Author of the Year) is one of the most popular children's writers working today. His hugely successful Alex Rider series[1] has sold over ten million copies worldwide[2] and won numerous awards[3], including the Children's Book of the Year Award for ARK ANGEL at the British Book Awards and the Red House Children's Book Award for SKELETON KEY. He scripted the blockbuster movie[4] STORMBREAKER from his own novel[5], and also writes extensively[6] for TV, with programmes including MIDSOMER MURDERS, COLLISION, INJUSTICE and FOYLE'S WAR. Anthony Horowitz is the author of THE HOUSE OF SILK: THE NEW SHERLOCK HOLMES NOVEL. He is married to television producer Jill Green and lives in Clerkenwell with his two sons, Nicholas and Cassian, and the ghost[7] of their dog, Lucky.

www.anthonyhorowitz.com

ANTONY JOHNSTON, who wrote the script for this book, is a veteran author of comics[8] and graphic novels[9], from superheroes such as DAREDEVIL and WOLVERINE, to science-fiction adventures like WASTELAND and DEAD SPACE, and even thrillers such as THE COLDEST CITY and JULIUS. He also writes videogames, including many of the DEAD SPACE series, and other games like BINARY DOMAIN and XCOM. His debut fiction novel[10] FRIGHTENING CURVES won an IPPY award for Best Horror. Antony lives in North-West England with his partner[11] Marcia, his dogs Connor and Rosie, and far too many gadgets with apples printed on them.

www.antonyjohnston.com

The artwork[12] in this graphic novel is the work of two artists, **KANAKO DAMERUM** and **YUZURU TAKASAKI**, who collaborate on every illustration. Although living on opposite sides of the globe, these Japanese sisters work seamlessly[13] together via the Internet.

Living and working in Tokyo, **YUZURU** produced all the line work[14] for these illustrations using traditional means[15]. The quality of her draughtsmanship[16] comes from years of honing her skills[17] in the highly competitive world of manga.

KANAKO lives and works out of[18] her studio in London. She managed and directed the project as well as colouring and rendering the artwork digitally[19] using her wealth of knowledge in graphic design.

www.manga-media.com
www.thorogood.net

1. série Alex Rider qui a connu un immense succès

2. dans le monde

3. a reçu de nombreux prix

4. a écrit le scénario du film à grand succès

5. à partir de son roman

6. beaucoup

7. fantôme

8. bandes dessinées

9. de romans graphiques

10. premier roman

11. compagne

12. L'illustration

13. de façon homogène

14. tous les dessins au trait

15. moyens

16. coup de crayon

17. pendant lesquelles elle a peaufiné sa technique

18. travaille dans

19. la numérisation de l'illustration

Collect all the Alex Rider graphic novels

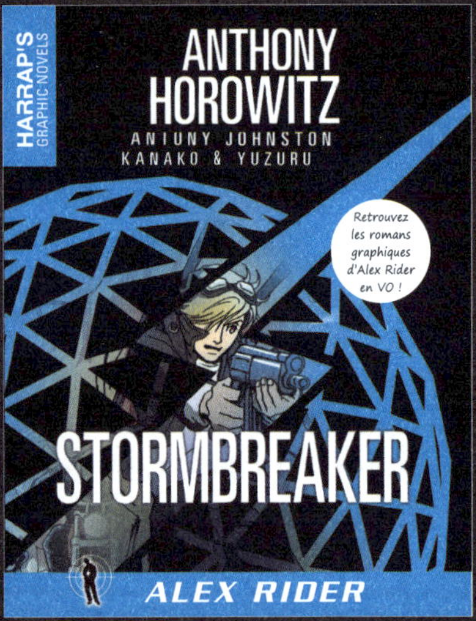
HARRAP'S
GRAPHIC NOVELS
ANTHONY
HOROWITZ
ANTONY JOHNSTON
KANAKO & YUZURU
Retrouvez les romans graphiques d'Alex Rider en VO !
STORMBREAKER
ALEX RIDER

HARRAP'S
GRAPHIC NOVELS
ANTHONY
HOROWITZ
ANTONY JOHNSTON
KANAKO & YUZURU
Retrouvez les romans graphiques d'Alex Rider en VO !
POINT BLANC
ALEX RIDER

HARRAP'S
GRAPHIC NOVELS
ANTHONY
HOROWITZ
ANTONY JOHNSTON
KANAKO & YUZURU
Retrouvez les romans graphiques d'Alex Rider en VO !
SKELETON KEY
ALEX RIDER

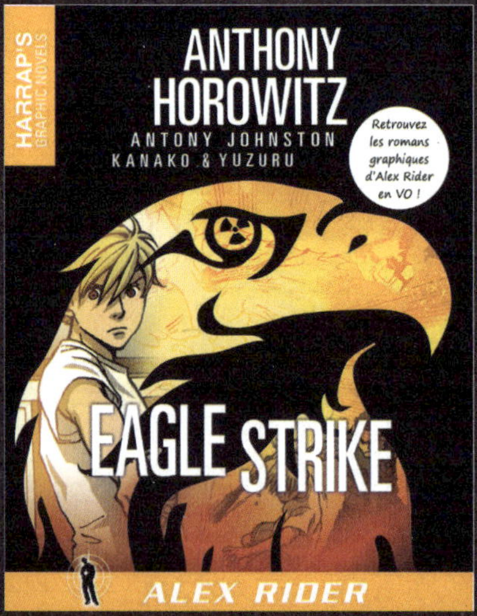
HARRAP'S
GRAPHIC NOVELS
ANTHONY
HOROWITZ
ANTONY JOHNSTON
KANAKO & YUZURU
Retrouvez les romans graphiques d'Alex Rider en VO !
EAGLE STRIKE
ALEX RIDER

Dépôt legal : août 2014
Imprimé en Espagne par Graficas Estella
314453-01/11026813 - Août 2014